AMBUSH RANGE

Center Point
Large Print

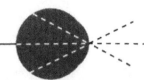
This Large Print Book carries the Seal of Approval of N.A.V.H.

AMBUSH RANGE

JACK BARTON

CENTER POINT LARGE PRINT
THORNDIKE, MAINE

This Center Point Large Print edition
is published in the year 2023 by arrangement with
Golden West Inc.

Copyright © 1955 by Joseph L. Chadwick.

All rights reserved.

Originally published in the US by Popular Library.

The text of this Large Print edition is unabridged.
In other aspects, this book may vary
from the original edition.
Printed in the United States of America
on permanent paper sourced using
environmentally responsible foresting methods.
Set in 16-point Times New Roman type.

ISBN 978-1-63808-698-7 (hardcover)
ISBN 978-1-63808-702-1 (paperback)

The Library of Congress has cataloged this record
under Library of Congress Control Number: 2022951542

CHAPTER ONE

Just west of Beaver Creek's second aimless crossing of the Texas line, a herd of six hundred snaky, saber-horned cattle plodded into the Neutral Strip and pointed northwest. Since the Strip was also known as No Man's Land, some of the trail hands entered it with apprehension, but after three days of riding through country that resembled the familiar Texas Panhandle, they overcame their unease.

The cattle wore Jim Bannister's J-Bar-B brand, and were driven by Bannister's ragtag crew of Mexicans and stove-in old cowpunchers who couldn't find steady jobs. The remuda was too small and the chuckwagon had long ago seen its best days. It was a raggedy-pants outfit.

Jim Bannister would have admitted as much. But since it was his first outfit, his first try at being his own boss, he would have made the admission with a measure of pride.

However, this drive in late summer of '87 wasn't his first try as a trail boss. Bannister had trailed more than one herd to Dodge City, taken another to Colorado over the Goodnight-Loving Trail, and made numerous short drives. He knew his job, and experience had taught him that a good trail boss makes sure of the lay of the land through which he drives. Having scouted ahead, he reined in atop a prairie swell, toward sundown of his third day in the Strip, and waited for the outfit to catch up.

There was water a mile ahead, and a bedground. Beyond lay a wide cedar brake and a stretch of sand flats. The rough country troubled him not at all, for the herd would be through it, barring accident, in a half-day's drive. Tomorrow would do it. Tomorrow the outfit would reach Boot Creek, its destination.

He relaxed in the saddle, hooking his right leg about the horn, and took out makings. He rode a thin zebra-dun gelding that drooped wearily. Bannister himself was gaunted. This drive had started down on the Llano, far across Texas, but for Jim Bannister the long, hard trail had its beginning many years ago, and had done a lot of twisting since.

He never talked of that trail, but he thought about it now as he rolled and lighted his cigarette. He would be thirty his next birthday, and he'd been a kid of but fourteen or fifteen when he made up his mind that he would end up a cowman rather than a cowhand.

Even at the start, he had known the trail would be hard. The era of free range overrun with mavericks, when all a man needed for a start in the cattle business was a long rope and a running iron, had passed before his time. Nowadays a man needed money—capital, the established cattlemen called it. A man working for other men, for thirty or forty dollars a month, had no chance of raising the necessary capital. He got to be a tophand, then, if lucky, a foreman. He saved some of his wages each month. It was a long, slow process, and during it he wasted his youth. No, not wasted it, but spent it. Bannister corrected himself on that. He worked with horses and cattle and men, learning. And it was the learning, rather than the mere owning of an outfit, that changed a man from a cowhand into a cowman. Capital and savvy. Both had been hard come by, but now he had his own outfit, such as it was.

Point of the herd half a mile away, chuckwagon a little ahead and remuda off to one side, the drive came on, the bawling of the cattle bringing music to Bannister's ears. He dragged hard on his cigarette, dog tired but content. From the corner of his eye, he saw a horseman emerge from the cedar thicket.

He turned his head to watch the rider, noting first that he was well mounted on a stocky sorrel, and second that there was a stoop to his shoulders and gray in his close-trimmed beard. Coming on at a brisk walk, the stranger climbed the little rise and reined in beside Bannister. Behind the beard, the man's face looked as craggy as ancient, eroded rock. But his eyes were a clear, lively blue. A man old in years, Bannister judged, but not in spirit. The old-timer folded his gnarled hands on his saddle-horn and peered toward the oncoming herd.

"Your outfit?"

"That's right."

"Headed where?"

"Boot Creek."

"Aiming to squat there?"

"Aiming to found a ranch there," Bannister said. Sensing that the old man was not merely idly curious, he felt on the defensive. "I bought Ed Akers' place."

"Bought it, did you?"

"That's it. For a hundred dollars."

"Akers cleared out a year ago."

Bannister nodded. "I know. I came down this way from Dodge last summer. I ran into Akers. I'd known him in Texas, years ago. He told me he was thinking of moving his herd out of the Strip. I took a swing around his range and liked what I saw. Just what I'd been looking for."

"So you bought him out for a hundred dollars?"

"For a quit-claim on his ranch headquarters."

"You got cheated, mister." The old man looked directly at him for the first time. "What did you say your name is?"

"I'd have said 'Jim Bannister' if you'd asked."

"Jubal Kane. Like I said, Jim, you got cheated."

Bannister puffed on his cigarette, trying to

see again with his mind's eye what the Akers' place—his place now—was like. A one-room house and a small barn with a corral off to one side of it. Buildings of sod, like all the buildings he'd seen during his trip through the Strip a year ago. People built shelters of what materials were at hand on any frontier, and here in No Man's Land, an almost treeless country, they used prairie sod just as Border Texans used adobe. A lot of work went into cutting the sod into chunks and laying the chunks like bricks to form walls. Of course, a small outlay of money had to be figured in, because doors and window sashes were necessities. They cost a price if made up, and lumber cost something if a man did his own carpentry work. Bannister's feeling was that, for a mere hundred dollars, he'd come by a bargain.

He said so.

Jubal Kane said, "Akers didn't tell you why he was clearing out?"

"He had a wife down in Texas. He didn't want to bring her into the Strip."

"As good an excuse as any. But not the right one."

"Well, what was the right one?"

"Akers ran up against some trouble," Kane said. "Another outfit claims the Boot Creek range. He was told he was squatting, and ordered to clear out. You must have happened along before he got out, and he was tricky enough to sell you his buildings. Buildings on another outfit's range. He swindled you, Bannister."

Bannister frowned. "That's not how I see it. Nobody owns any land here. Not even homesteader claims are any good. There are no courts to give anybody any title to the land. With buildings, it's different. What a man builds, he owns—and can sell. What's this outfit claiming the Boot Creek range?"

"Crescent."

"A big outfit?"

"Big and tough, Bannister."

Bannister glanced at the brand on the right shoulder of Kane's sorrel. It was a quarter-moon mark, a crescent. He said, "Kane, you wouldn't be Crescent's owner, would you?"

Kane showed a miserly smile. "Just one of its hands," he said. "The bigwigs at Crescent heard a strange outfit was coming into the country and sent me to find out what was up. Want some friendly advice, Bannister?"

Bannister deadened his cigarette against the sole of his boot, then straightened in the saddle. He swung the dun around so that he faced Kane. "I'm listening," he said. "Say your piece."

"Don't stop at Boot Creek."

"Thanks. But that's not advice I can take."

"Too bad," Kane said. "You're sure to get booted out. I wasn't told to give you a warning. I'm doing this out of the goodness of my heart.

You can't buck the Crescent Cattle Company. Like you said, there's no courts to give anybody any title to the land. But there's no law, either, to protect a man wanting to share the range. You savvy?"

"I savvy. But I don't scare as easy as Ed Akers."

"Could be that Akers was more smart than scared."

"All the same, old man, I'm moving into my buildings at Boot Creek."

Kane shrugged. "That's up to you," he said. "But later on, when the going gets rough, remember that an old man tried to get you to be reasonable."

He lifted his reins, turned the sorrel away. Once down from the rise, he headed north at a lope.

Bannister stared after him. No Man's Land had a reputation as a wild, lawless place, but he hadn't anticipated this kind of trouble. He'd bought the ranch headquarters at Boot Creek on sudden impulse, but after returning to Texas he'd made inquiries of a United States marshal and a Federal judge. Both had assured him that there was no legal ownership of land in the Strip. Unattached to any state or territory, overlooked by Congress when the boundaries of the western states and territories were established, the Neutral Strip was a vast area, one hundred sixty-seven miles long and thirty-four and a half wide, and the land remained open for those who could put it to use. According to what Bannister had been told, the only title to land here was actual possession. And no one man or outfit could keep actual possession of more than a small portion of so vast a range.

He knew that it wasn't overcrowded like the Texas cattle ranges. Only a limited number of cattlemen had ventured into the Strip. The uncertain future of the country, and its notoriety as a refuge for rustlers, horse thieves and other outlaws had kept the cattlemen cautious. Most had set up mere camps rather than permanent ranch headquarters, and some had pulled up stakes and cleared out after the blizzard of '86 caused them ruinous losses in stock.

So there should be room for me, Bannister reflected. Room for J-Bar-B *and* Crescent.

Still, convincing the Crescent outfit might be tough. He'd sized up Jubal Kane as a truthful sort, and he didn't doubt that the old man's employers would make the going rough for anybody moving onto the Boot Creek range. It occurred to him that he could find graze and water beyond the range Crescent claimed, but then he dismissed the thought. If he let himself be pushed off one range, sooner or later he'd let himself be pushed off another.

Moreover, those buildings at Boot Creek belonged to him. He'd bought them and for a whole year he'd dreamed of the day when he'd move into them. He wouldn't let that dream come to nothing.

He put Jubal Kane's warning out of his mind and rode down to join his outfit. Tomorrow he would lead it to Boot Creek.

They showed up the next morning, when the J-Bar-B herd was midway through the sand flats. Bannister sighted them topping a dune half a mile away, and reined in to watch them. One of his crew, Will Langley, swung over from point of the herd.

"Trouble, Jim?"

"Yeah."

"What kind?"

Bannister hadn't told Langley and the other trail hands about his talk with Kane. He'd seen no reason to, for he hadn't expected Crescent to move against him until after he established himself at Boot Creek, paid off the crew and started them back to Texas. He couldn't expect them to side him in this sort of trouble. He was paying them less than standard trail wages—a thing he regretted but couldn't help—and so he couldn't call upon them to do more than make the drive. Actually, he doubted that they'd be much help in a fight even if he did pay them fighting wages. His crew consisted of Mexicans, some mere kids and none real vaqueros, and Texans either too old or too shiftless to be worth much.

Some didn't even own firearms. Will Langley seemed the best of the lot, but even he couldn't be considered a tophand. Langley had done some bronc-busting down in the Big Bend a couple of years ago; he'd never been the same since a mustang fell on him.

Bannister said, "An outfit called Crescent claims the Boot Creek range. They'll try to turn us back."

"And if we don't turn back?"

"Maybe they'll try to turn us."

"How far will you be turned, Jim?"

Bannister saw an earnest speculation in Langley's eyes. Physically, Will Langley was but a shell of the man he'd once been. His stiff left leg gave him great pain on occasion and his left hand could do little more than hold a pair of reins. All he had left was spirit, Bannister thought.

He said, "Will, I don't know. This came a little too sudden, before I could get set." He watched the approaching riders. "Seven to one. Tough odds."

"Make the odds seven to two," Langley said. "That's not too bad, if we work it right. They'll want to talk at the start. That'll be in our favor. I'll stay a little distance behind you and cover you. Let the hombre ramrodding the bunch know I'll drop him if they make a move against you."

Bannister eyed him questioningly.

Langley smiled. "I can handle a Winchester."

"That wasn't in my mind. I was wondering why you want to sit in on the game."

"You're paying my wages."

"Damn skimpy wages," Bannister said. "Well, I'm grateful—and we'll give it a try."

The riders swung west of the herd, pulling up in a line abreast. Old Miguel Aragon, the coosie, brought his chuckwagon to a halt midway between them and point of the herd. Bannister rode out, a pressure of excitement building up in him.

When he and Langley came within easy rifle range of the Crescent riders, Langley reined in, dismounted and turned his horse sideways to the seven. Then, in Texas Ranger fashion, he rested the barrel of his rifle across the saddle. Bannister halted fifty yards from the group, and one Crescent man came out to face him.

Bannister knew this must be one of Crescent's bigwigs, as old Jubal Kane called them, for he rode with an air of self-importance which ordinary ranch hands never affected. Bannister saw arrogance in him, and toughness to back it up. He was a burly man about forty, his bulk seemingly all hard-muscled brawn. He halted ten feet from Bannister, a scowl on his ruddy face.

"I'm Matt Harbeson. You the owner of this outfit?"

"I'm the owner. Bannister's my name."

"Got a quit-claim for Ed Akers' house and barn, have you?"

"That's right."

"It cost you a hundred dollars, I hear." Harbeson didn't wait for a reply, but pulled a roll of bills from his shirt pocket. "Here's two hundred. Hand over the quit-claim, and you've earned yourself a hundred percent profit on your investment."

Bannister shook his head. "I'm not selling out, Harbeson. Not for two hundred, not for two thousand. Put your money back in your pocket."

"You've got no choice," Harbeson said. "You'll take this money and you'll clear out. That's the way it's to be."

He flung the roll of currency at Bannister. It struck him on the chest. It broke open and bills showered to the ground.

"You've been bought out, Bannister," Harbeson said. "I've got six witnesses to the deal. Now turn back the way you came. If I catch you west of these sand flats, you'll wish to hell you'd never come into No Man's Land. Pick up your money and get started."

"It's still your money. You pick it up."

As he spoke, Bannister saw two of Harbeson's men leave the group. One rode out to flank him from the right, the other to flank him from the left. He lifted the dun's reins, pulled it to one side so that he was no longer directly between Harbeson and Will Langley's rifle. A faint breeze toyed with the money on the ground, carrying bills away like tumbleweeds.

Bannister said, "That rifle behind me is beading you, friend. It'll drop you if those riders come any closer."

Harbeson glanced at Langley. He showed no fear, but he flushed angrily. He raised a hand in signal to his flankers. The one off to Bannister's right, a middle-aged man, halted at once. The other, a young tough, kept walking his horse toward Bannister. His right hand rested on the butt of his holstered gun. Harbeson gestured again.

"Pull up, Sherry. Pull up!"

The young rider halted reluctantly. He called, "I can take him, Matt. If that hombre with the rifle is bothering you, I can take him too."

"Quit it," Harbeson yelled. "Quit it, I tell you!"

"All right, Matt," Sherry said. "Whatever you want."

Bannister looked back at Harbeson. "This should be a lesson to you. Next time don't bring a boy along to do a man's job. It could get you killed. Now get down and pick up your money, or ride out without it."

Harbeson was worrying about Sherry, still watching him. A look of alarm spread over his face. He shouted, "Sherry, you fool!"

Even as he shouted, a shot from Sherry's gun slammed across the sand flats in a sharp blast of sound.

CHAPTER TWO

As Harbeson's alarmed shout blended with the report of Sherry's gun, Jim Bannister slapped leather. Whipping the gun across his middle to bead the young hardcase, he heard Will Langley cut loose with his rifle. The sickening sound of Langley's slug tearing into flesh and bone brought another cry from Matt Harbeson. From the corner of his eye, Bannister saw the Crescent boss going down with his horse.

He caught Sherry in his Colt's sights, but the range was too long for a hand gun. Despite his wild streak, the Sherry kid hadn't been fool enough to rely on his revolver. He'd grabbed out his carbine, dropped from his horse and fired from flat on the ground. Sherry made a difficult target, and Bannister knew he would miss the kid even as he squeezed the trigger.

But Sherry also had missed his first shot at Langley, and Langley had fired at Harbeson. Bannister saw the kid readying another shot at Langley, so he drove a second slug at Sherry. It came close enough to startle the youth and bring him twisting around on his belly to level his rifle at Bannister. By now Bannister had his horse in motion. He raked it with his spurs, drove it toward the Crescent man. Sherry fired, but with too much haste, and as he jacked another cartridge into the firing chamber, Bannister came within hand gun range.

He fired. Sherry's yelp echoed the shot. The young hardcase lost his rifle and lay writhing. Bannister reined his horse about, heading back toward Matt Harbeson. Langley's shot had caught Harbeson's horse in the head, killing the animal instantly. Harbeson had tried to leap clear, but still lay with one leg pinned beneath the dead horse.

Beyond Harbeson, the man who'd flanked Bannister on his right now held his hands shoulder high and looked anxiously in Will Langley's direction. The remaining four Crescent men were moving in, slowly and with caution. Bannister swung over to where their boss lay helpless and beaded him with his cocked gun.

"Keep them out of it, Harbeson."

Harbeson swore, but then he shouted an order at the four. They halted at a distance, willingly enough. It was over, much to Bannister's surprise. He needed a little time to recover his mental balance and understand how he and Langley had come out of it alive against such odds. He heard Sherry moaning out there, and called to Jubal Kane. The old-timer rode in, a miserly smile on his bearded face.

"If I hadn't seen it, I'd never believe it happened," Kane said. "You'll take some booting, bucko."

He reached for his catch-rope, shook out the loop and made his throw. He caught the horn of the dead horse's saddle, turned his sorrel away and slowly took up the rope's slack. The sorrel strained mightily, lifting the weight of the dead animal from Harbeson's leg. Harbeson dragged himself clear, and Kane returned and removed his loop. Coiling the rope, he watched Bannister in a half amused, half admiring way for a moment, then rode off to see the wounded Sherry.

Harbeson picked himself up, nearly fell when his left leg buckled, and recovered his balance. He stood there, his face stiff to mask the pain, but staring at Bannister without trying to hide the hatred in his eyes.

Kane returned shortly with Sherry's skewbald pony in tow. He reined in close to his boss. "Need help to mount, Matt?"

Harbeson said, "When I need help, I'll ask for it," and put foot to stirrup. A spasm twisted his features as his injured leg bore all his weight, but he rose to the saddle.

Kane said, "Sherry's got a slug through his right arm, Matt."

Harbeson said, "To hell with Sherry." He had his murky gaze on Bannister again. "This doesn't change a thing, mister. Don't let me catch you west of these sand flats."

He wheeled the paint horse about and rode off at a hard lope. Three of his men followed him.

Kane motioned to the man still frozen by the threat of Will Langley's rifle. "Charlie, come give me a hand with that fool Sherry."

He got down and removed the rigging from the dead horse, placing it among some rocks a little distance away. Then he and Charlie went to Sherry. They worked on him a little while, bandaging his wound with his neckerchief, and got him onto Charlie's horse. Charlie mounted behind Sherry, and they set out in the direction the others had taken. But Jubal Kane stopped beside Bannister.

Bannister said, "More advice, old man?"

"Sound advice, Bannister. Don't stretch your luck too far."

"I won't trust to luck from now on."

"That would be smart," Kane said, and rode out.

Bannister joined Will Langley. He said, "Thanks, Will. It worked out fine, but you took too big a chance firing at their boss instead of that punk kid. If his aim had been a little better, he'd have downed you."

"I knew that," Langley said. "But I'd told you how I'd play it and I figured you'd be counting on me."

He booted his rifle and mounted his horse. Because of his crippled arm and leg, rising to the saddle required great effort. He said, "What now? Do we go on?"

Bannister nodded.

"Well, a man must do what he plans, I guess. But, look—are you keeping any of us with you once you're settled at Boot Creek?"

"I can't pay wages, Will. Not at the start."

"Alone, you won't have a chance against that crowd."

"I'll give them a fight, anyway."

Langley was lost in thought for a moment. Then he said, "I'm staying on. You can pay me later. A year from now, if that's the best you can do. Keep me in grub and tobacco and you've got yourself a hand." He smiled wryly. "It won't be a one-sided deal. I've got no job back in Texas, and I'm not likely to find one that would suit me. I'm a riding man, Jim, and I don't want to hire out as a livery stable hostler or a saloon swamper. It's a deal?"

"Stay until the going gets rough," Bannister said.

They rode back toward the herd. The crew had halted the drive upon hearing gunfire, and now they stood in an uneasy bunch near the chuckwagon.

Bannister said, "All right, let's move out," but old Jeb Hadley said, "What are we getting into, Bannister?"

"Not a thing," Bannister told them all. "The trouble's been taken care of, and there'll be no more until after the herd is at Boot Creek. Get it there in a hurry and I'll pay you off so you can clear out."

He ordered Miguel Aragon to move on with the chuckwagon. Then, with the rig under way, he rode with Langley toward the scattered cattle. The others came along reluctantly, and shortly the herd strung out on the move. The cattle handled easily here on the barren flats, since there was no grass to encourage drifting, and by high noon the outfit struck a stretch of rocky, broken country that finally sloped away into a broad brush-grown hollow. Riding ahead, Bannister made his way through the hollow with its dense thickets of briar, grapevines, wild currant and plum bushes. Once clear of the brush he reined in and gazed across the Boot Creek country.

It was a wide strip of undulating prairie with natural drift fences. Here to the east lay rough terrain: brush thickets, rock fields, sand flats. To the north rose a range of craggy bluffs. To the west and south, but far in the distance, were low rimming hills. A man would need to string little barbed wire to enclose this range. Boot Creek flowed from the hills to the west and twisted its way to the center of the range, then turned north to a gap in the range of bluffs.

The buildings stood close to the creek with their backs to the bluffs, and by standing in his stirrups Bannister could see their roofs. He started toward them, but he halted again when he came close enough to have a full view of the sod house and barn.

Smoke was rising from the pipe chimney of the house.

It startled him, yet he realized that he should have expected Crescent to occupy the place. In fact, it would have been more sensible for Crescent to hold the buildings than to make its play out on the sand flats. Why hadn't Harbeson done that at the start?

Then it occurred to him that Harbeson might not have thought of such a move. Somebody else might be holding down the place, squatting there without Crescent's knowledge. He hoped so, and he started toward the buildings once more.

He saw three horses in the corral adjoining the barn. He aimed directly toward the pen, and stopped by it. He found three saddles draped across the top bar of the pole fence, one in fair condition and the others disreputable from age and hard usage. They were not the sort of saddles men with jobs would use. The horses were fine looking animals, however, though not in the Crescent iron. The gray carried a Running W, the blaze-faced black a Lazy B. He couldn't make out the bay's mark, and had a hunch it wasn't a quarter-moon. He felt a small measure of relief, knowing he wouldn't have to buck that outfit so soon again. At the same time he realized that whoever squatted here would also give him trouble. Squatters were always a stubborn lot. He rode into the yard, toward the house. A man appeared at the open doorway, a tin cup in his hand.

"Howdy, stranger."

Bannister reined in facing him, and nodded. He was a stocky, coarsely handsome man of about twenty-five with rust-red hair and china blue eyes. He smiled amiably enough, but Bannister judged him to be a tough hand.

"Step down, friend," the man invited. "Come in and have chuck."

"Thanks, but I've eaten."

"That's something. A rider in this country turning down a handout meal." The squatter drained his cup. Then he said, "Pat Keough's my name. Come on in and meet my partner. He's one of the Maugher boys. If you're not hungry, maybe you're thirsty. We've got a jug cached away." He grinned hugely, teeth gleaming in the bronze of his face. "Real good forty-rod."

Bannister eyed him warily. Keough seemed too anxious to get him inside. During his earlier trip through the Neutral Strip, he'd been impressed by the hostility of the people he met in cow camps and homesteader places and a grubby settlement or two along the way. The denizens of No Man's Land had been suspicious of him, a stranger, and he'd felt that none of them trusted the other. So

Keough's friendliness didn't exactly assay as pure gold.

Also, the man had spoken of his partner—indicating one companion—yet there were three horses in the corral and three saddles on the fence. Bannister kept his face expressionless, but Keough sensed his uneasiness.

"What's wrong, friend? You leery of me and my partner?"

"Should I be?"

"Naw. Jake and me, we're as easy to get along with as any two hombres can be."

Jake Maugher appeared behind Keough, and Keough, after tossing his cup inside, stepped down from the doorway. Maugher followed him outside and leaned against the sod wall of the house with his thumbs hooked in his gunbelt. He was a dour-faced scare-crow of a man, rail-thin and shabbily dressed. No Man's Land was a poverty-stricken country, Bannister knew, but Jake Maugher looked more down on his luck than most of its people. He stared at Bannister in a covert fashion, his jaws working on a tobacco cud.

Keough said, "You're Bannister, ain't you?"

The question took Bannister by surprise. "That's right. Who told you about me?"

"A little bird, maybe."

"You're quite a joker, Pat."

Keough chuckled. "Jake and I met Matt

26

Harbeson on our way home today. He told us that there'd be a hombre named Bannister along to claim we were squatters here."

"Been living here long?"

"A real long time, bucko. Two, three hours."

Bannister frowned, aware that the next move was his and not liking the way Keough had put it up to him. He could clear out or make a fight of it. Or it could be that they wouldn't let him ride out. He examined the amiable face of Pat Keough and the dour face of Jake Maugher, and he knew. He wasn't supposed to ride out. Harbeson had made a deal with them, and they meant to finish him off—these two and the third one.

He said, "How much is Harbeson paying you, Keough?"

"Two hundred."

"Not a lot of money, considering the risk you're running."

"Not a lot of money for a Texan, maybe, but to us Strip hombres it's plenty." Keough continued to smile, but his eyes were cold and calculating now. "Harbeson said you were fast with a gun. Think you're fast enough to take Jake and me?"

Bannister shrugged. "Maybe you two, but not three. Where's the third man, Keough? In the barn, with a cocked gun lined on my back?"

He didn't wait for a reply, but jabbed spurs to his dun. The horse bounded toward Pat Keough, and a gun opened up from inside the barn.

CHAPTER THREE

Bannister heard the shriek of the slug, then Keough's yelp as the dun rammed into him. Grabbing his rifle from its boot, Bannister flung himself from the still moving horse and plunged through the doorway of the house. He stumbled, sprawled on the rammed-earth floor inside, and a second shot from the barn passed over him to strike somewhere within the house. He heaved over in a roll, and came to his knees against the thick sod wall. He worked the Winchester's lever and leveled the barrel by the door jamb. Catching a glimpse of a man within the dimness of the barn, he lined him in his sights.

The man fired again. The slug tore splinters from the door jamb. Bannister drove his shot across the yard and heard the report echoed by a scream. The man there jerked grotesquely, then pitched forward onto his face, half in and half out of the barn. He did not move again.

A sort of agonized cry came from Jake Maugher, and he came into Bannister's range of vision. Maugher took several running steps toward the downed man, realized his danger, stopped short and swung toward Bannister. His revolver came up, but he was badly rattled. Seeing the rifle boring at him, he suddenly lost his nerve. He froze with his weapon still not quite beading Bannister, as easy a mark as an inanimate target.

Bannister said, "Drop it, Jake. Drop it."

Maugher dropped the gun, cursing bitterly.

Bannister said, "Now move to the middle of the yard." He waited until the man obeyed, then shouted, "Keough! You, Keough!"

"Here, Bannister. I'm right here."

"Going to see it through?"

"Naw. I've seen enough."

"Throw your gun out where I can see it, then get out there with Jake."

Keough's six-shooter came flipping out from the side of the house. It dropped close to where Maugher's weapon lay, and then Keough appeared and joined his companion in the center of the yard. Bannister stepped from the house, picked up the guns and threw them inside. Circling wide about the pair, he went to the corral. He pulled a Winchester from one saddle, an old Army Springfield from another. He tossed them onto the roof of the barn. Turning, he saw Jake Maugher staring at the dead man in a shocked, disbelieving way.

He gestured with his rifle. "You, Keough," he said. "Saddle your horses."

Keough moved toward the corral, Maugher toward the dead man.

Keough got a rope off one of the saddles, and

said, while shaking out the loop, "That's Russ Maugher, Jake's brother. He's taking it hard."

That was true. Jake Maugher was on his knees, turning the body over onto its back. Bannister heard him utter a sound much like a sob.

"The three of you knew the risks you ran."

"Yeah. I reckon bushwhacking's not our game."

"What is your game?"

"Me, I deal in livestock—horses and mules." Keough seemed not at all shaken by the shooting and Russ Maugher's death. He still had his easy grin. "Business hasn't been so good lately. So when Harbeson made us his offer, we jumped at it—like three damn fools."

"The Maughers are horse thieves, too?"

"They deal in cattle mostly."

"All right," Bannister said. "Get those horses saddled."

He crossed the yard and leaned his rifle against the wall of the house. He hunkered down, took out makings. Jake Maugher was still kneeling beside his dead brother. By the time Bannister smoked his cigarette short, Keough came from the corral with the three horses in tow. No word was spoken by Keough and Maugher. They wrapped the dead man in a blanket, lifted him onto the bay horse, and used a catch-rope to secure the body across the saddle. Maugher mounted the gray, caught up the bay's reins and looked at Bannister, his face ugly with rage and hatred.

"You should have killed me when you had the chance," he said. "Because I'll be back, Bannister!"

Bannister said nothing.

Maugher rode out, swinging over to the creek and turning north along it. Bannister looked after him, feeling a little sorry for him—and wondering if these buildings were worth a man's life. It was easy to think otherwise, but considering it at greater length, he decided that the buildings had nothing to do with it. A man placed the real value on his own life. Russ Maugher hadn't cared about the buildings at all. He'd been willing to gamble with his life for a share of Matt Harbeson's two hundred dollars, and he'd lost exactly what he'd gambled.

Mounted now, on the blaze-faced black, Keough rode slowly toward Bannister, who threw away his cigarette and rose. Keough reined in, eyeing him uncertainly.

"I guess it would be asking too much, eh, Bannister?"

"You're not getting your guns back, Keough."

"I suppose not." Keough still held his horse there. "I won't be back, bucko. I want no more trouble with you. But Jake wasn't fooling. When he comes back, he'll not come alone. He'll bring some more Maughers with him. There's a lot of them here in the Strip."

"I'll watch out for them."

"Them and the Crescent crowd, eh?"

Bannister nodded. "Where's Crescent headquarters located, Keough?"

"Seven or eight miles northeast of here," Keough said. "Aiming to pay Harbeson a visit?"

"If that crowd doesn't leave me alone. Is Harbeson head man there?"

"There's a manager, a tenderfoot sent out by the company owning Crescent Ranch. But Harbeson is the man you've got to worry about."

"What's he there, just the ranch boss?"

"He's on the payroll as foreman, but hell, he *is* Crescent."

"What's the manager's name?"

"John Forbes," Keough said. "If you go to Crescent to see him, bucko, take plenty of your own men along. Crescent's sure a cross-dog outfit."

He rode after Jake Maugher, a cocky hardcase on a stolen horse. He had a bedroll tied behind his saddle, and no doubt it contained all he owned in the world. Outside the Strip, Pat Keough would almost certainly finish up at the end of a rope, but so long as there was a No Man's Land he could get by.

Bannister entered the house and took stock of the place. It was much as he remembered, furnished spartan-fashion. A stove at one end, a pair of bunks at the other, a plank table and benches in the center. It had an empty, unused look, since Ed Akers had moved his personal gear out when he left. There was a battered coffee pot on the stove, but Bannister supposed it had belonged to the Maughers or to Pat Keough. A film of dust covered everything, and, like all sod buildings, the house was utterly gloomy. Still, once he washed the two windows at the ends of the room, more light would filter in to dispel some of the gloom. He could find no fault with the place. After all, a sod house offered good shelter, being cool in summer and warm in winter, and this was the first house he had ever owned. It looked fine to his eyes. He went outside, picked up his rifle and mounted his horse.

Riding to meet his outfit, he found it trailing through the brush-tangled hollow. In another hour, the herd moved onto the Boot Creek range and the cattle were turned loose to scatter.

Miguel Aragon already had a meal on the fire, and while the trail hands waited for chuck, Bannister paid them off. Each man who had come to him without a mount at the start of the drive was permitted to keep a horse out of the remuda. After they'd eaten, they tied their bedrolls behind their saddles and mounted. Then, with a brief "so long" or "*adios*" from each, they rode out.

Only Will Langley remained.

Bannister said, "Will, you'd better understand what you're letting yourself in for." He told Langley about the Maughers and Pat Keough.

"Jake Maugher will want to even up for his brother. That means we'll be feuding with an outlaw crowd as well as fighting a range war with Crescent."

"I'll stick."

"All right. I wish I had a dozen more like you."

"There's only one thing I don't like," Langley said. "Our having to sit and wait for the trouble to come hunting us. I'd rather go out and meet it halfway. That would give us more of a chance of holding on here."

Bannister nodded. "I've been thinking of that," he said. "Tomorrow I'm riding to Crescent headquarters and have a talk with the head man there."

"That's not likely to do any good."

"The outfit's managed by a tenderfoot," Bannister said. "Maybe I can throw a scare into him that will get Crescent off our necks. Anyway, it can't make matters worse than they are. Let's drive the chuckwagon to headquarters. I want to move our gear and provisions into the house before dark."

He set out alone in the morning, riding with more caution than haste. He saw two small groups of riders along the way, but in the distance. He passed scattered bunches of cattle, riding close enough to one bunch to see the Crescent brand. At midmorning, just after circling a clump of blackjacks, he came within sight of the ranch headquarters.

The buildings were of frame, painted white with green trim, and stood in a neat group at the base of a small hill. Not even in Texas had Bannister seen a more imposing ranch headquarters. Two things were evident: Crescent had built to stay, and there was plenty of money behind the outfit.

Drawing close, Bannister was puzzled by the maneuvering of a buckboard and team near the buildings. The rig kept going around and around in a small circle on a grassy flat. The buckboard was shiny black with gleaming yellow wheels, drawn by a team of matched, high-stepping grays. A man stood off to one side, watching intently. And now Bannister saw that the driver of the rig was a woman.

He pulled up, and it was a sight worth watching. The brightly painted buckboard, the fine horses in fancy harness, the handsome and fashionably attired woman handling the reins, made a startling picture here in No Man's Land.

The woman handled the reins awkwardly, he saw. She sat rigidly erect, every inch of her tense. Strain showed in the set expression of her face. He understood then. She was just learning to drive a team. That explained her endless driving around the flat and her being watched by the man, a cowhand, whose saddled mount stood handy in case she let the horses get away from her.

Her circle widened slightly each time around, and now, as she neared the spot where Bannister sat his horse, the right wheels dropped into a gully hidden in the high grass. An experienced driver would scarcely have noticed the sudden sideward lurch, but the woman uttered a startled shriek and hauled back on the reins so sharply that the grays came to a rearing stop. This frightened her even more, and she sawed on the reins, crying, "Whoa—whoa, there!" in great alarm. The horses came down but, spooked at the rough handling of the ribbons and the fright in her voice, continued to prance and plunge. Their confusion, plus the sharp tilt of the buckboard, was edging the woman toward panic.

Bannister walked his dun in on the grays, talking to them. "Steady, boys. Steady." He leaned from the saddle, caught the near animal by its headstall with his left hand and stroked its arched neck with his right. "Steady, there, you handsome devil. Steady!" He glanced at the woman, and said, in the same soothing tone, "Ease up a little on the reins."

She obeyed, and the near horse quieted almost immediately. The off animal quit his carrying on with a final snort. The cowpuncher had mounted and now he came loping across the flat. He was not one of the Crescent hands who had cut Bannister's trail in the sand flats, but a stranger. He pulled up alongside the buckboard.

"You all right, Mrs. Forbes?"

She said shakily, "I—I'm not quite sure, Dick. What's happened? This buckboard seems about to go over onto its side."

"The right wheels are in a gully, that's all."

"It won't go over?"

"No, ma'am," Dick said. "Wait, and I'll get you out of there."

He swung around to the opposite side of the buckboard and started to step from his horse to the rig.

Bannister said, "Friend, let the lady get it out, herself."

The Crescent man already had swung his right leg over the saddle-horn. He held himself sideways on his horse, staring at Bannister. He was young and had a hot-tempered air about him.

He said, "Listen you, I got orders not to let Mrs. Forbes get hurt."

"She won't get hurt," Bannister said. "Let her get herself out of the fix she's in."

"What the hell for?"

"So she learns to handle the team. Which she won't, if somebody takes it over every time she makes a mistake."

"Now, look here, mister—"

The woman said, "He's right, Dick. I mustn't give up every time I'm frightened." She looked at Bannister. "You're sure I'll get out all right?"

37

Bannister nodded, studying her more closely. She might not be truly beautiful, but she was one of those women who could, without design or effort, sharpen a man's awareness that he was a man. He judged her to be in her late twenties, an auburn-haired woman with a flawless complexion and finely molded features. She wore a riding habit of some dark green material, a jaunty brown hat and gloves to match it. This, in a country where other women wore calico dresses and sunbonnets.

He said, "You'll get out all right. But ease up on the reins. You're pulling too hard on them, hurting your horses. Relax. Lean against the seat back. You're trying too hard. Go on now, lean back."

She did as he told her, but gingerly.

He said, "Stay like that, Mrs. Forbes. Keep telling yourself those grays aren't going to get away with you. They can't get away, with Dick and me here. All right?"

She smiled. "All right."

She slapped lightly with the reins, as Dick must have taught her, and called, "Giddap!" The grays started out, and the buckboard, coming from the gully, righted to even keel. She drove a short distance, then halted the team and looked around. "How was that?"

Bannister swung over to her. "Just fine," he said. "Now just keep in mind that you've got to keep yourself and your team relaxed. Can you do it?"

"Why, yes. Yes, I think I can now. You're a good teacher, Mr.—"

"Bannister is my name, Mrs. Forbes."

"Bannister?" Her eyes widened. "The Texas gunman?"

"Gunman? I've never been called that before."

"But you're the man who—"

"Who had trouble with Matt Harbeson and those other Crescent hands?" He nodded. "I'm the man."

Dick rode in on him, saying, "I was wondering about you, hombre. What do you want here?"

"Not trouble," Bannister told him. "So pull back."

Dick stared, angry and defiant. Then, evidently not liking the glint in Bannister's eyes, he reined his horse away a few feet.

Bannister looked back at the woman. "I'd like to see your husband, Mrs. Forbes. At least, I understand that a man named Forbes is the manager of this outfit,—and I want to see him. Where will I find him?"

"I'll take you to him."

"I said I don't want trouble." He smiled. "You don't trust me?"

"I'll be honest with you," she said. "No I don't trust you. Matt Harbeson couldn't be mistaken about you. His horse was killed under him and

39

one of the men was shot. That's proof enough that you're—well, dangerous."

She waited for no reply but drove toward the ranch buildings, Bannister riding beside the rig and the disgruntled Dick coming along behind it. She handled the team easily enough, being preoccupied and relaxed. She halted the grays before the steps of the ranch house porch, and Dick dismounted to take the reins. Bannister made haste to get down and help her from the buckboard. She gave him a chill "Thank you," and quickly turned away.

He followed her up the steps, noticing the fine set of her shoulders and the way her red-brown hair curled at the nape of her neck and how small-waisted she was. She crossed the porch, opened the door, entered the house. By the time he stepped inside and closed the door, she had crossed the hall and entered a room which was so comfortably furnished that it seemed more like a study than a ranch office.

The hallway was wide with a straight-backed chair or two against the wall, and a wall mirror, and a clothes-tree in a corner. Brussels red carpeting ran along the hall and up the staircase. He looked around, impressed, and thought, this is what being a cowman can lead to, a house like this. Then he reminded himself that in the cattle business a man needed a great deal of luck, since it was, after all, more of a gamble than anything else. He was a long way from a house like this, perhaps half a lifetime away.

He entered the study. Its chairs and sofa were upholstered in dark red leather and book-laden shelves covered one whole wall. The man who sat behind the desk surprised Bannister. Somehow he had taken it for granted that the woman would have a young and robust husband. But Forbes was middle-aged, a rather frail appearing man by cow country standards, gray of hair and mustache and pallid of complexion.

He did not rise or offer his hand. "So you're Bannister, are you?"

"That's right," Bannister said, in the same barely civil tone. "And you're Forbes, I take it."

"Another brash Texan," Forbes said, glancing at his wife. "What is it you want of me, Bannister?"

"I want you to call off Harbeson and your crew."

"You're asking for something I can't do."

"I'm not asking, I'm telling you."

Forbes took a cigar from a humidor on the desk. He clipped its tip with the blade of a small knife fastened to his watch chain. His movements were deliberate, and Bannister imagined women would consider him handsome. He looked well-groomed, freshly shaved, his mustache close-trimmed. He wore a gray tweed suit with a white shirt and maroon string tie. He might have been taking his ease in some country manor a thousand miles from No Man's Land. To Jim Bannister it was incredible that such people as the Forbeses should be living in the Neutral Strip. His cigar lighted, Forbes cocked an inquiring eye at Bannister.

"You're telling me, are you?"

"That's it," Bannister said. "I'm holding you responsible for the actions of the Crescent hands. If they come gunning for me again, I'm coming gunning for you. Do we understand each other, Mr. Forbes?"

CHAPTER FOUR

Forbes's reaction was a mocking smile. "Could anyone possibly misunderstand you, Bannister?" he said. His wife was patently frightened, however, and she moved around the desk to stand beside him. She said, "John, this man is dangerous. He means what he says."

He glanced at her, frowning. "I know, Helen. But what can I do about it? Explain to him that I have no control over Harbeson and the crew? You can't explain to a man like him."

Because of the woman, Bannister said, "If you have an explanation, now's the time to make it. Talk up, man. What do you mean, you've got no control over Harbeson and the crew? You're the ranch manager, aren't you?"

"I look after the ranch's business affairs," Forbes said. "Matt Harbeson is in charge of the actual operation of the outfit. I was sent out here several months after Harbeson founded the ranch, and I had orders not to interfere with him. Which is only reasonable, since I'm not a cattleman."

Bannister said, "He goes a lot farther than a mere ranch foreman needs to go."

"Well, he's not just a ranch foreman."

"No? What is he, then?"

"He has a stake in Crescent Ranch, one beyond his wages," Forbes said. "The company owns another ranch, in Wyoming. Harbeson founded it, and he did such a good job that the company rewarded him with a block of Crescent Cattle Company stock. He'll be rewarded with more stock when this ranch is a going enterprise. Or rather, when he's worked out all the company's plans for it." He paused, puffing on his cigar. "Plans with which you're interfering, Bannister. I'll show you what I mean."

He rose, turned to a map on the wall behind the desk.

It was a large, hand-drawn map of the Neutral Strip. It was the first such map Jim Bannister had seen, and until now the boundaries of the country had been hazy in his mind. He saw how the Strip was bounded by Texas on the south, New Mexico on the west, Oklahoma Territory on the east, Kansas and Colorado on the north. The few settlements were marked. The courses of the Cimarron River, Beaver Creek and the streams feeding the latter were traced. He noted the location of Crescent Ranch headquarters, and, squared off about it, in red ink, a large portion of the surrounding range. Also, he did not fail to notice that Boot Creek range lay within the red-gridded area.

Forbes traced the red fine with a finger. "The company has decided on controlling all the land within this section, Bannister. Plans call for fencing it with barbed wire next spring. Meanwhile, Matt Harbeson has orders to keep out other cow outfits and the homesteaders. Since Boot Creek is in the heart of the section, you—"

"Crescent can't get away with it," Bannister cut in. "This land is in the public domain if any land ever was."

"Possession is nine-tenths of the law, friend."

"You're taking too much for granted. Your company hasn't got possession. No outfit can hold so much land when there are no courts to back up its claim. Harbeson may think it can be done with a crew of gunhands, but he's as wrong as a man can be."

Forbes shrugged. "You'll have to convince him of that."

"No. You'll have to convince him. I told you I'm holding you responsible."

"And I told you I have no control over him."

"Then you'd better get in touch with the men who give him orders," Bannister said. "Where's this Crescent Cattle Company have its headquarters?"

"Philadelphia. The company officers and most of the stockholders live there." Forbes's voice had sharpened. "It will do no good for me to contact the home office, Bannister. The company heads have given Harbeson a free hand and nothing I can say or do will change it. But you'll not believe that. I said there's no explaining to a man like you."

His wife said, "John, make him an offer. It's foolish to defy such a man."

Forbes pondered briefly, then said, "Bannister, would a thousand dollars change your mind about settling at Boot Creek?"

"No."

"Well, name a price."

"I've got none."

"Nonsense. Everybody has a price. Name yours."

"All right," Bannister said. "A dollar more than Crescent can pay."

Forbes flushed. "Bannister, I'm a businessman and therefore accustomed to talking sensibly. If you won't be reasonable, we may as well bring this discussion to an end. You've threatened me with violence. Very well. I'll take steps to protect myself. Don't come here again unless you're prepared to suffer the consequences."

Bannister nodded. "Just so we understand each other," he said, and left the room.

He was descending the porch steps when he saw the young hardcase, Sherry, in the doorway of the bunkhouse across the yard. Sherry's right arm rested in a sling, but he had a gun in his left hand and a look of pure hatred in his eyes. The second Crescent hand, Dick, stood midway between the bunkhouse and the barn with his gaze shifting back and forth between Sherry and Bannister.

Bannister halted on the bottom step, taking Sherry's measure.

Someone came from the house, crossed the porch, stood above and behind him. He sensed that it was Helen Forbes, and considering her no threat, he continued to watch Sherry. The range across the wide yard was too great for accurate shooting with a hand gun, and it didn't seem likely that the tough Crescent man was left-handed. Sherry's aim should be wide of its mark if he opened fire now. On the other hand, he just might make a lucky shot. Dick might have to be reckoned with, too, though at the moment he had a look of uncertainty about him.

Bannister said, "Don't try it, Sherry. It's too risky."

"I'll take the risk, damn you." Sherry's voice lifted to an angry shout. "I can drop you before you get your gun out!"

Mrs. Forbes called, "No, Sherry—no!"

He glanced at her, and the instant his gaze shifted Bannister leaped for his horse and grabbed his rifle from its boot. He worked the lever as he swung around and immediately brought the weapon up to bead the man in the doorway.

The woman cried, "Sherry!" And Dick said, "Lay off, Sherry. He'll kill you, you fool!"

Sherry swore, but then he eased down the hammer, and thrust the gun into the waistband of his Levi's. He said, with a weak show of bravado,

"Another time, mister," and backed into the bunkhouse, kicking the door shut. Dick turned away when Bannister gave him a challenging look, and disappeared into the barn.

Bannister booted his rifle, swung to the saddle and walked the dun over to the steps. "You wanted to say something to me, Mrs. Forbes?"

She regarded him with intense dislike. "What is it with you?" she asked. "Do you enjoy this sort of thing?"

"I don't enjoy it. I'm not spoiling for a fight."

"Then why don't you be reasonable?"

He folded his hands on the saddle-horn and leaned forward. "Mrs. Forbes, I made plans for a ranch of my own a long time before Crescent came into this country. I decided a year ago that it would be at Boot Creek, and that's where it's going to be. If I've got to be a gunman and fight, that's how it will be." As an afterthought, he said, "But I'm sorry if I frighten you, Mrs. Forbes."

"You do frighten me."

"Then you'd better get your husband to control Matt Harbeson."

"I? How can I do anything about such a situation?"

"You must have some influence over your husband," he said. "A woman like you."

Deep color stained her cheeks. "I'll do what I can, but let's not bring personalities into it."

"Sorry. I wouldn't have got personal, but you

asked how you could do anything about the situation. I merely pointed out—"

"Whether or not I have influence over my husband is none of your business," she cut in. "Now I wish you'd leave, before I lose my temper and get down to personalities. I doubt very much that you'd want to hear what I think of you."

He said, "I doubt it, too," and, touching his hat to her, he turned away.

Standing there on the porch, watching the Texan ride out, Helen Forbes realized that a part of her anger was directed at herself. She had become emotionally upset under Bannister's too intimate scrutiny and his brash "a woman like you." It embarrassed her to have a man other than her husband reveal that he had appraised her as a woman. Bannister had also made her conscious of him as an individual male, perhaps by design, and it annoyed her to know that he had succeeded. He had stepped out of bounds.

She disliked him for what he was, and feared him too. A year had passed since John and she came West, and in that period she had learned that No Man's Land attracted many dangerous men. According to her husband, several men on Crescent's payroll were a bit too expert with their guns, and she sensed that Matt Harbeson had a vicious side to his nature. She accepted them, conceding that such men might be necessary to the success of a ranch in such a country. But Bannister—she feared Bannister. He was Crescent's enemy.

She had wondered about him before his visit, curious as to what sort of man dared defy Harbeson and his riders. Harbeson had returned from the encounter with Bannister in the sand flats and given her husband only a garbled account of what happened. John had been forced to get the truth from Jubal Kane, and the old man said, in her hearing, "That Texan is bad medicine." Yes, she had wondered about Bannister. And now she knew.

He was a dangerous man, in more ways than one. A woman would have to be on guard against him. He was hard to the core, yet he possessed a sort of fascination, a capacity to make her think of him as a powerful, magnetic male. She felt a small sense of guilt, as though she had for a fleeting moment forgotten that she was a married woman. She hoped she'd seen and heard the last of Jim Bannister—and she knew the hope was false.

She went inside and found her husband seated at his desk, a troubled frown on his face. It occurred to her that John Forbes was inadequate to deal with such men as Jim Bannister and Matt Harbeson, and then she felt ashamed of the disloyal thought.

She said, "John, what will you do?"

He rose and began pacing to and fro. "There's not much I can do," he said. "Bannister won't move away from Boot Creek, and Harbeson will have no rest until he's moved him out—or one or the other is killed. I'll have to arm myself and get Harbeson to keep a couple of men on guard here at headquarters."

"You've got to report the situation to the company, John."

"Little good that will do. The company heads have too much faith in Harbeson. They believe he can do no harm."

"They'll have to believe he can, if you say so," Helen said. "After all, you're a stockholder as well as ranch manager. And your brother Ben is—"

He halted by the window, and in the glare of sunlight his face looked haggard. "I'm a minority stockholder," he said. "As for my brother, Ben Forbes is secretary of the Crescent Cattle Company—and a damn greedy man. I can't imagine him being concerned about bloodshed here, or even about the danger to me. All he wants is for this ranch to show a profit, a big profit."

"You may be doing him an injustice, John."

"No. I know that brother of mine."

"What about Mr. Delong, the president of the company?"

"He's like Ben."

"And the treasurer, old Mr. Vorhees?" Helen said. "I met him once, and he seems like a fine old gentleman. I can't imagine him sanctioning bloodshed." She saw a spark of interest in her husband's eyes. "He's not greedy, John. He's a banker, and already wealthy. Besides, his word is law with the others. Let him know what's happening here, John!"

"Well, I could write to him."

"A letter would be too long on the way," she said. "And there's not much time. It's got to be a telegram."

"A telegram? The nearest telegraph office is at the railroad up in Kansas."

"We'll send Dick Mercer to Kansas with it."

"Well—"

"Write out the message, John," Helen said, knowing now what she had suspected all along—that she was the stronger willed of the two.

CHAPTER FIVE

Keeping a sharp lookout for Crescent riders, Jim Bannister traveled southwest at an easy lope. He intended to run rather than fight, if he encountered any of the outfit, because this wasn't the time or place for him to be drawn into a showdown. He must choose less open country and a day when the element of surprise was with him. Fight he would have to, eventually, but he intended to risk it only when he had some chance of winning.

No good had come of his visit to Crescent headquarters. John Forbes had told the truth: he had no control over the activities of Matt Harbeson and the crew. More, he had no hope that the man could get the company's bigwigs to restrain Harbeson. They had too much at stake. In the light of their grandiose plans, they would back their foreman to the limit in order to protect their investment. So the threat Bannister had made against Forbes was an empty one. The man was a weakling, and he couldn't use violence against a man unable to defend himself.

Some transplanted Easterners adapted themselves to the rugged life of the cattle country, but John Forbes wouldn't. He simply didn't count in the scheme of things, and his only value to the Crescent Cattle Company, it seemed, was an ability to handle finances, make deals, keep accounts. The man's show of defiance had been mere sham. Within himself, Forbes must conceal more than a little fear of the Matt Harbesons and Jim Bannisters of No Man's Land.

Still, Bannister had his curiosity about the ranch manager. He wondered what had brought Forbes West, and decided that it must have been some failure, or at least a lack of success, back East. The man was past his prime, at an age where only failure could have caused him to come to a country in which he would always be an alien. On the other hand, there was his wife to be considered. It seemed to Bannister that such a woman, strikingly attractive and apparently intelligent, would not have married a man nearly twice her age if he were a ne'er-do-well and wholly inadequate. He wondered if Forbes had hoodwinked him, after all. Still, whatever John Forbes might be, it was Matt Harbeson and his tough crew he would have to fight.

He reached the broken country bordering his Boot Creek range without sighting riders, and shortly, riding along the base of the bluffs, he saw his buildings. After the visit to Crescent, his own house looked utterly squalid. Sod walls, dirt roofs, earth floors. . . . Well, he wouldn't always live so poorly. Give him ten years, and he'd have a house as fine as John Forbes's. With a woman in it, maybe. A voice in Bannister's mind asked: A woman like Helen Forbes? He didn't know about that. Women like her were a rarity in the cattle country; indeed, such women didn't belong in the cattle country. A man might wish for a handsome, fashionable, hothouse variety of woman, but he'd do well to plan on marrying one more suited to withstand the rigors of ranch life. And the truth must be faced—for a long while, he couldn't afford any kind of wife.

He saw Langley's horse in the corral, but nothing of Will himself. It seemed odd that Langley didn't appear in the yard to see who was approaching. Since he understood the danger of their situation, it seemed so odd that Bannister felt a sharp uneasiness. He reined in, studied the buildings and the surrounding range. He saw nothing out of order, but his uneasiness didn't abate. Langley's failure to show himself meant that something had happened.

Bannister knew of two things that could have gone wrong. Either Crescent riders had come here, or Jake Maugher had returned, and Langley had been unable to handle the trouble. Riding on, Bannister circled the place. He came around to the old chuckwagon which stood at the north side of the barn, and then he saw Langley. His body was bare to the belt, and his back was a mass of bloody welts. They had bound his wrists to a rear wheel, and he hung there, not quite on his knees, unconscious.

Riding in and dismounting, Bannister saw the whip on the ground. They had used the whip off the wagon, Bannister's own whip. He got out his pocketknife, cut the ropes binding Langley's wrists to the wheel. Langley fell away, sprawled loosely.

Bannister lifted him, carried him to the house, placed him on one of the bunks. Langley groaned and began to thrash about.

Bannister said, "Easy, Will, easy," and held him down when he struggled to get from the bunk. After a long moment, Langley became fully conscious. He lay still, then, his face smeared with blood, sweat and dirt They'd given him more than a beating. They'd tortured him.

"Who was it, Will?"

"Crescent."

"All right. We'll pay them back. Take it easy and I'll doctor you up." Bannister rummaged through the store of supplies they'd moved into the house until he found a bottle of carbolic acid. He heated water in a basin, made a carbolic solution. Using an old flour sack, he washed Langley's battered face and then had him lie on his stomach while he cleansed the lash-torn flesh of his back. The whip had been wielded by an expert and every blow had left its bloody mark.

Bannister said, "Who used the whip, Will? Harbeson? The man whose horse you killed out on the sand flats?"

"No, a man they called Sanchez. But Harbeson did the counting." Langley rolled over, sat up. "Forty lashes. I felt every one. I didn't pass out until after they left." He held his head in his hands. "Four of them from the east, along the bluffs. I held my gun on them. They wanted to know where you were. They kept talking, giving the others a chance to come in and take me from behind. The other four came from the north, through that gap in the bluffs. They had me boxed, and it seemed sensible to drop my gun."

"What then, Will?"

"I got Harbeson's gun in my face, twice. Just hard enough to stun me. I went down to my hands and knees. A couple of them got off their horses and grabbed me. They tied me to the chuckwagon, and then Harbeson gave me a lecture—damn him!"

Bannister took out makings, rolled a cigarette and offered it to Langley. Will shook his head. His color was bad, a gray pallor. Bannister worried about him.

"Harbeson said he was giving me a chance to be sensible," Langley went on. "He said he was going to teach me a lesson, and it had better be one for you too. He told me to clear out—out of No Man's Land—and to take you with me." He swore weakly but bitterly. "Then this Sanchez used the whip."

Bannister lighted the cigarette and dragged

hard on it. The smoke tasted foul, for some reason. He went to the door and threw the cigarette outside. He went to the stove, found a handful of hot embers in it, and added sticks of kindling. He filled the coffee pot, set it on to heat. He turned and watched Langley from across the room, and by the time the coffee was ready, he'd made up his mind. He filled a tin cup and took it to Langley. Holding it with both hands, Langley tried to drink. He gagged on the coffee, however, and handed the cup back to Bannister.

Bannister said, "Will, you're clearing out."

"Like hell I am. I've got a score to settle with that crowd."

"They weren't as rough with you as they could have been. If Harbeson had really had it in for you, I'd be digging your grave now."

"So I should feel good about that?"

"Will, you look like a sick man," Bannister said. "You won't be yourself again by the time they come back—which may be tonight, after Harbeson finds out I was at Crescent today. If they come back, I don't want to be here. I'm going to play it smart and be hard to get at— unless you do the fool thing and force me to stay and try to protect you." He shook his head. "Give me my chance, Will. Without you to worry about, I'll have it. And with a little luck, I'll even the score for you and for myself."

Langley said sourly, "I was supposed to give you a hand."

Bannister nodded. "You were, until this happened. And I'm grateful. But now, the shape you're in, you're a burden to me."

"I'll be myself again tomorrow."

"Here's hoping you are. But neither of us will be here tomorrow."

"Have it your way. Where are we going?"

"Into the rough country, where we'll be hard to get at," Bannister said. "You get some rest until I've got an outfit together and the horses ready."

Outside, he mounted the striped dun and cut for the Crescent riders' sign beyond the buildings. They'd headed north along Boot Creek, toward the gap in the bluffs: that explained his not having seen them on his way back from Crescent headquarters. They favored another, no doubt shorter trail. He forded the creek, turning south across the range. Ten minutes later he sighted the remuda. He removed his rope from his saddle-horn as he rode toward the horses. Deciding on a little gray, he shook out the loop and closed in to make a throw. The horses wheeled away, but after a short chase he had the gray at the end of the rope. He led it to the buildings, left it tied to the dun's saddle-horn. Entering the house, he found Langley stretched out on the bunk.

Langley said, "You're right, Jim. I'm a sick man."

"Can you stand to make a little trip?"

"I'll have to stand it, won't I?"

Bannister said, "I guess you will," and regarded him with concern. Langley's face was no longer pale but flushed, and Bannister, touching his forehead, felt the heat of a high fever. "It won't be a long one," he said, knowing that it couldn't be for Will Langley.

He gathered together as many provisions as would make a fair-sized pack for the gray. He added a skillet and a coffee pot. Lacking a pack-saddle, he got a piece of canvas off the chuckwagon and bundled the stuff into it. He carried it outside and tied it onto the gray. He roped and saddled Langley's horse, a blue roan gelding, and led it from the corral to the other animals. He went inside, found a spare shirt in Langley's warsack, and helped him don it. He gathered Langley's and his own gear, then rolled their bedding. He tied his own bedroll behind the dun's saddle, and Langley's behind the roan's.

Langley came out, walking unsteadily, and Bannister helped him onto the roan. He said, "You see my gun and hat anywhere, Jim?"

Bannister found both in the middle of the yard, where the Crescent men had beaten Langley to the ground. He gave them to Langley, and a few minutes later they rode out, Bannister leading the pack-horse.

He looked back at the buildings, frowning and

bleak of eyes. He was being driven from his home. He had to admit that. Telling himself he would come back made him feel no better, for whether he did or not depended on how he made out in the inevitable showdown with Crescent. He knew the odds against him. What Harbeson and his men had done to Will Langley proved that he was bucking a crowd which would show no quarter. He supposed hanging on was foolhardy, but it stood to reason that the Crescent outfit must have a weak spot somewhere—and with luck he might find it.

He headed south, Langley coming along behind him, slack in the saddle, his shoulders sagging and his head tipped forward so that his chin rested on his chest. He was able to keep up only because Bannister held his dun and the pack-horse to a slow walk.

At Crescent that evening, Helen Forbes sat down in the parlor after dinner with a bit of crocheting. She felt restless, as she so often did, and needed to keep at least her hands busy. But every few minutes her needles became idle and she sat lost in thought. By turning her head slightly, she could see into her husband's study across the hall. He was pacing the floor as he always did when troubled. They had not spoken of it, but both knew they were waiting for something to happen.

It happened finally: the heavy thump of boot heels as a man crossed the porch, the noisy opening and closing of the door as he entered the house, more footsteps across the hallway, and then at the study doorway, the voice saying, "John, I want a word with you."

Helen disliked many things about Matt Harbeson. She hated his habit of entering the house—their house—without knocking whenever he felt like it, and the lack of respect in his voice when he spoke to her husband made her squirm. She disliked the way he often looked at her, too, with a mocking smile and easy familiarity in his eyes, as though he had some intimate knowledge of her and was amused by it. She had puzzled about his manner toward her for a long time, and finally decided that behind it lay nothing more than his fancying himself more of a man than John Forbes—and his imagining that she too believed such a thing. Matt Harbeson was an inordinately vain man.

She lay aside her crocheting, rose and walked to the hall doorway. Ordinarily, she would not have stooped to eavesdropping, and she never concerned herself with the affairs of the ranch except as they involved her husband personally. But she knew why Harbeson had come to the house tonight, and she expected a clash between him and John. She wanted to hear everything said between them. She could see them facing each other, Harbeson so big that he dwarfed John Forbes.

Harbeson was saying, "Sherry says you sent Dick Mercer to Kansas with a telegram. How come?"

"I want the company to know the situation here, Matt. This trouble with Bannister—"

"It's not trouble I can't handle," Harbeson cut in. "Bannister kept only one man with him at Boot Creek, and that one's been taken care of. If that Texan has any sense at all, he'll take it as a warning and clear out. What the hell did he want here, anyway?"

"He came to threaten me," Forbes said. "He had an idea that my being ranch manager gave me control over you. I told him otherwise, but he still insisted that he'd hold me responsible for your actions. Hence my telegram to Philadelphia. I've got to protect myself as best I can."

Harbeson's tone mocked him. "As best you can! Hell, a lot of good that crowd back East will do you. Quit your meddling and let me take care of Bannister. If what happened to his hired hand doesn't send him back to Texas in a hurry, he's going to wish it had. I'm done fooling around with him. If he's not cleared out by tomorrow night I'm fixing him good. As for you, friend, don't go over my head again with any damn telegram!"

He swung around, came striding into the hall, and stopped short upon seeing Helen. He looked at her in that mocking way, smiling.

"Sherry tells me you kept him from shooting that Texan."

"Sherry is a little confused."

"Oh?"

"I kept him from being shot by the Texan."

"Maybe you did, at that. He's a punk, that Sherry, and no match for a tough hand like Bannister."

Harbeson's gaze traveled over her, and it seemed to Helen that he was, in his mind, stripping her of her clothing. Her flesh crawled.

He said, "Sherry says too that Bannister gave you pointers on how to handle a team. That was real nice of him. Maybe it gave you a good opinion of him, eh?"

She could not help saying, "I like him no better than I like you. My opinion is that he likes violence as much as you do. That makes him something of a brute, doesn't it?"

Harbeson scowled, then laughed loudly. He left the house still chuckling. John Forbes came into the hall as the door closed behind Harbeson. The foreman's rough talk had left him looking upset.

Helen said, "You did the right thing in sending that telegram, John. This proves it. Whatever he did to that hired hand, it won't drive out

Bannister. And I don't believe he'll get the best of Bannister." She paused, and a sudden anger seized her. "I almost wish Bannister would get the best of him!"

CHAPTER SIX

During the night Jim Bannister set the ailing Will Langley up in a camp deep in the south hills, and in the morning he left the hideout to travel through the rough country east of the Boot Creek range. He came within sight of his buildings at midmorning, and halted among some towering rocks at the edge of a brush thicket. He loosened the dun's cinch, and then, leaving the horse deep within the rocks, he took his rifle and settled himself in the shade of a boulder to keep watch. He had no plan of action other than to wait and see if Crescent came looking for him. He would decide upon his move when Harbeson and crew made theirs.

He saw no movement across the range except for the sluggish drifting of his own scattered cattle as they grazed. He had a view of the gap in the bluffs beyond his buildings, but no riders appeared through it. When, at noon, someone did show up, it was from the east. And not riders, but a single person with a buckboard and team.

The rig followed the base of the bluffs, and the gleam of yellow wheels in the bright sunlight told him that it was the one Mrs. Forbes had been driving the day before at Crescent headquarters. The distance was too great for him to identify the driver, and, remembering her trouble with the team, he doubted that it would be Mrs. Forbes. But at the same time he could not imagine John Forbes driving far from his headquarters, and after a few minutes of straining his eyes, he convinced himself that it was the wife after all.

But why, he wondered. Why?

It took her ten minutes to reach his ranch headquarters. She halted the team in the middle of the yard, and remained on the seat of the rig. He watched her until his eyes ached from the strain of peering so intently, and then he went to his horse. Riding across the open range, he kept watch for riders along the eastern bluffs or through the gap to the north, but none appeared. The woman waited there, wholly relaxed today and holding the grays without difficulty. He rode into the yard, halted beside the buckboard and removed his hat. Curiosity was eating at him, but he took pains to hide it.

"You learn fast," he said. "You handle your team like an expert today."

"You should have seen me back a mile or so. I wasn't so expert then."

"Have trouble in the rough country?"

"A little. But I remembered in time to keep relaxed."

"Good. Never let your horses sense that you're frightened." He replaced his hat and took out makings. While building a smoke, he waited for her to satisfy his curiosity. When she didn't, he said, after lighting up, "You didn't drive out here just to show me that you can handle your team—or to gaze upon my manly beauty."

"Hardly. I came to give you a warning."

"Oh?"

"Matt Harbeson will come here tonight, to drive you away."

"Or try to kill me?"

"Yes. That too, I suppose."

"Well, I've been expecting him," he said. "But thanks anyway for the warning. But you're not giving it to me gratis, are you?"

"I think you know why I'm warning you."

"It's not because you're concerned about me. Does your husband know?"

"No. I came without his knowledge."

"He's a lucky man, your husband. Few men in this country have wives to worry about their safety—or to bargain for their lives."

Helen flushed, and her voice sharpened. "He told you the truth. He has no control over Matt Harbeson. He's done the only thing he can to stop him from using violence against you—sent a telegram to a company officer informing him of the situation. I did come here to bargain for his life. I'm afraid that if Harbeson moves against you tonight, you'll carry out your threat against my husband. So I've given you a warning, and in return—"

"In return, I should withdraw my threat against John Forbes?"

"Harming him will gain you nothing."

He puffed on his cigarette, studying her. He was discovering something about her: she could weave a spell. Excitement rose in him. That was sheer folly, of course. She was another man's wife, and also a part of world so alien to his own that, even if she weren't married, they could have nothing in common. But he found himself thinking: *When I have a woman of my own, it's got to be one like her,* even when he could see—and almost feel—Helen Forbes's hatred of him.

She said, "Are you going to be decent about it, Bannister?"

"Quit your worrying, Mrs. Forbes."

"You mean—"

"I'm taking your word for it that Forbes can do nothing about Harbeson," he told her. "So put your mind at rest."

She studied him for a long moment, seeming to doubt his sincerity. But finally she said, "Thank you, Bannister. I must have known there was a decent side to your nature, else I wouldn't have come to you. Now that you know Harbeson and the crew are coming here, you don't intend to stay—do you?"

"Mrs. Forbes, I don't think you're able to understand a man like me," he said. "I told you yesterday that I'll fight Crescent if I have to. I haven't changed my mind. I won't be driven out."

"It seems so senseless."

"Not to me. Not to Matt Harbeson, either."

"But you have no chance of winning a fight with him."

He smiled. "I wouldn't fight if I didn't think I had a chance of winning. I think I've got two chances. One is that I may be able to make things so hot for Crescent that the crew will get a bellyful of fighting. The other is that sooner or later Matt Harbeson will make a mistake and let me get at him. When one or the other happens, I'll have Crescent whipped."

"You mean to kill Harbeson, don't you?"

"If he doesn't let up on me, yes."

She shuddered. "To deliberately plan such a thing seems—horrible."

He shrugged. "It's the way he wants it. And it's not anything new. It's the way of the cattle country when a new range is being opened. There's always some big outfit wanting control— and some little man wanting to share. Then it's dog eat dog."

"And you're not afraid, Bannister?"

He considered that, frowning. "Maybe I am, deep inside," he said. "I don't like gambling with my life. I don't even want to take a beating like Harbeson and his men gave my hired hand yesterday. But more, I don't want to live with the knowledge that I've been beaten and have lost what little I own. Does that make sense to you, Mrs. Forbes?"

"I don't know," she said. "I—"

He saw the look of alarm in her eyes the instant it appeared. She was staring at something beyond him. He twisted in the saddle and saw half a dozen riders coming in along the base of the bluffs, traveling at a lope and already within rifle range. They began spreading out to intercept him if he made an attempt to escape.

He looked at Helen Forbes.

She said, "I didn't know, Bannister."

She seemed genuinely distressed, and he believed her. He caught a movement to the north, and turned in that direction. Four riders emerged from the gap, one of them Matt Harbeson. These four also spread out, two fording the creek to head him off if he made a run for it. He was already hemmed in except toward the southwest, and he would be exposed if he headed in that direction. They would back-shoot him if he rode out.

He swung his horse one way and another, panic stirring in him. Then, convinced of the futility of flight, he held the dun steady and considered the sod house. He could fort up in it, put up a fight of sorts. But that would end with his being killed; they could keep their distance and sharpshoot until they finished him off. Before he could make up his mind what to do, it was too late. They closed the trap.

Helen said, "Bannister, save yourself!"

He saw with surprise that she meant it. "No chance," he said.

They ringed his headquarters, came into the yard. There was the old man, Jubal Kane, his gray-bearded face expressionless but his eyes sympathetic. There was big Matt Harbeson, grinning hugely. There were the others, as rough looking as men could look. They reined in, forming a circle about him and the woman.

Harbeson looked from Bannister to Helen, then back at him again. "Now ain't this something?" he said. "You and the dude's missus. I guess we know now why you gave her pointers on how to handle a team. So she could drive out to visit you. A fast worker, you."

"Don't imagine things, Harbeson."

"Don't need to. It's right before my eyes."

"Keep the lady out of it, I tell you."

"Sure," Harbeson said. "It's a scandal, but I won't tell it around." His amusement faded. He nodded at Jubal Kane. "Get his guns."

Kane gigged his horse forward, coming alongside Bannister. He took Bannister's revolver from its holster, his rifle from its boot. Swinging away, he threw the weapons into the barn. Some of the Crescent hands grinned wickedly, knowing what was going to happen to Bannister. Several eyed him with a lively speculation, wondering no doubt how much of a roughing-up he could take. Bannister felt his heart pounding hard and fast.

"Better get out of here," he told Helen Forbes.

She was frightened, and looked it. She gazed at Harbeson. "What are you going to do?"

"Well, I'll tell you, Mrs. Forbes," Harbeson said. "After I'm done with this man, no woman will be able to stomach his looks. It'll make you sick to look at him. I'm going to teach him to keep off Crescent range—and away from other men's wives."

Bannister said, "Drive out, Mrs. Forbes."

She said, in a hopeless voice, "Matt, don't."

Harbeson laughed. He glanced at a swarthy, lank-faced man. "Sanchez, you and Buck get him off that horse."

Sanchez rode in on Bannister, his gun in his hand and ugly eagerness in his dark eyes. He was followed by a ruddy-faced blond man who didn't seem quite so eager. Sanchez jabbed spurs to his mount, and it bounded forward. He clubbed at Bannister with his gun, but Bannister ducked so that Sanchez, missing the blow, was defenseless for an instant. Bannister clouted him hard to the face, causing him to cry out and reel in the saddle. Wheeling his horse about, Bannister came alongside Buck and drove a blow at him. Buck took it on the jaw, his head rocking back and a grunt escaping him. He recovered instantly, however, and grappled with Bannister. They were straining against each other when Sanchez came alongside and rapped Bannister at the back of the neck with the barrel of his gun.

The pain numbed Bannister. Then Buck jerked him from the saddle and he dropped to the ground. He landed heavily, lay sprawled for a moment. Then he struggled to rise, and got help from the two men. Off their horses now, each caught him by an arm and hauled him to his feet. He struggled to break free, but they wrenched his arms around behind him. Helpless, he watched Harbeson dismount and come toward him.

Harbeson said, "You were given plenty of chance to clear out, Bannister. So don't cry about this." He brought his right hand up, slapping Bannister hard across the face. "We'd have let you move out with your cattle, bucko, but you wouldn't have it that way." He slapped again, with his left hand. "Now you'll leave empty-handed. And next time you'll sure know better than to play a game you can't win."

Bannister heard Helen Forbes cry out, but her words were lost to him under the weight of Harbeson's next blow. This time it was not with an open hand, but with a clenched fist. It slammed against his mouth, and he had the sudden taste of blood. Another punch caught him over the heart, with such force that he would have gone down if Sanchez and Buck hadn't held him.

That was the beginning. Harbeson battered him methodically. The man's heavy face grew sweaty with effort. Bannister saw the blows launched, felt their impact. It was a beating without mercy, with each blow gauged so that it punished but did not let him escape the torture into unconsciousness. He felt as if he were being torn apart, and still it went on and on.

CHAPTER SEVEN

It ended when Matt Harbeson became winded, when his arms tired and his fists ached. They dumped Bannister to the ground, and for a little while granted him a respite. In his agony he wondered if it would not have been better to shoot it out with them, to have died quickly instead of by inches.

They stood over him, talked about him. He sensed their nearness, heard the muttering of their voices. He saw nothing but a red-black mist which did not exist except behind his eyes. Finally, rough hands seized him again and splintering pain returned. They hauled him to his feet, boosted him upwards, and he realized fuzzily that they were putting him astride a horse. He wanted to cry out against this, for in his nightmare of pain he was a dying man, and a dying man could not sit a horse. But he could not cry out; he no longer had a voice.

He toppled from the saddle, against one or more of them, and dropped to the ground. One swore, and booted him hard to the head. There was one last explosion of pain, and then nothing at all.

He regained his senses to a degree some time later. At least sufficiently to become aware that he was going to live, that pain alone was not death. He realized that he was tied on a horse which was being led by another rider. Gradually, his mind became clear enough for him to make use of his senses. He saw the back of the rider: Sanchez. He heard another rider coming along behind him. They were traveling at an easy lope, and heading into the sand flats. His wrists were tied to his saddle-horn. A rope rigged around his shoulders and running beneath the belly of his horse held him erect.

They rode deep into the sand flats, and finally the rider behind Bannister said, "This ought to be far enough." It was the blond man, Buck.

Sanchez reined in and said, "Yeah, I guess so." He knotted the ends of the dun's reins and draped them about the animal's neck. He stared at Bannister and said, with a wicked satisfaction, "Damn, but he's a mess!"

"He'll look worse before he's done for." Buck's voice was uneasy. "A lot worse."

"Well, you won't have to look at him then."

"It's a hell of a thing, Sanchez. Let's untie him and give him a chance."

"Nothing doing," Sanchez said. "We've got our orders."

He removed his rope from his saddle, cut Bannister's dun across the rump with it. He rode along as the dun started out, slapping again and again with the rope and yelling to spook the horse, halting only when it was heading south across the wasteland at a hard run.

The dun ran until its sides heaved, then slowed to a walk. For a time, Bannister was too dazed to understand his danger. He knew that he was free of his torturers, and that alone mattered. When realization came, he strained at his bonds, and then, finding no give in them, he tried to stop the horse with his voice. He could utter only incoherent sounds. The dun continued to travel southward across the seemingly endless sand. The sun beat down upon Bannister's bare head. Its glare reflected from the sand into his pain-filled eyes.

Despair took hold of him. Buck had been right. It was a hell of a way to die, tied to the back of a horse headed nowhere. . . .

Late in the afternoon, the sudden motionlessness of the horse aroused him from a stupor. They had reached grass, and the dun had stopped to graze. There was grassland ahead and to either side as far as the eye reached. And nothing else. No cow camps, no homesteader places. He was no better off than he'd been in the barren sand flats.

The dun wanted to graze, but the tied-back reins kept it from lowering its head. The horse was in as difficult a position as Bannister.

He tried the ropes binding his wrists to the saddle-horn, but there was still no slack in them. He worked his shoulders, but this served only to drive hammer blows of pain through his battered body. He noticed that the rope pulled on the calf of his right leg each time he moved his shoulders, however, so he tried working from that direction. He slipped his foot from the stirrup, placed his weight on the left stirrup, and finally, after several minutes of clumsy, painful maneuvering, he got his right leg untangled from the rope. The entire rigging about him and the horse loosened, and by shrugging his shoulders, at the expense of pain, he worked the rope off himself.

He considered next the greater problem of his bound wrists. The dun kept shaking and tossing its head against the reins, and Bannister decided to do something about them before tackling his tied wrists. He bent forward and took one of the leather straps between his teeth.

There was little strength and much pain in his jaws, but after an eternity of gnawing the line parted and the dun could lower its head. Grazing, the horse stood more or less motionless and Bannister gave his attention to the rope about his wrists. He could see no way to free them except by using his teeth, and so, with great effort, he swung his right leg over the horse's rump and slipped his left leg from its stirrup. His knees buckled when his feet touched the ground, and for a long moment he hung against the horse. Finally, forcing his legs to hold him, he stretched his lanky body and began worrying the knot of the rope with his teeth.

Another eternity of time passed, and occasionally it seemed hopeless. The knot slipped finally, so suddenly that he lost his balance and fell away from the horse. He sprawled loosely on the ground. It was good to be there. He sank into a coma.

It was dusk when he awoke—or rather, since it had not been a real sleep, when he regained his senses. He had the feeling that he was not alone, and he levered himself up on his elbows to look around. He saw a man hunkered down about twenty feet away, puffing on a pipe. It was the Crescent hand, Jubal Kane. Unable to support himself for long, Bannister sank back and stared up at the darkening sky.

He said, "Well, get it over with, why don't you?"

Kane rose and came to stand over him. He knocked the embers from his pipe by tapping the bowl against the palm of his left hand. "Bannister, I've been wondering how you got off that horse," he said. "It couldn't have been done without help. And you had no help. I know. I cut for sign, and there's none but yours."

"Don't let it worry you, old man."

"Nobody needs to worry about you, I reckon."

"Still, they sent you to make sure I didn't get off my horse, didn't they?"

"Who? Harbeson?"

"Who else?"

Kane shook his head. "If Matt had figured there was a chance of you getting loose, he wouldn't have sent me. Sanchez, maybe. Or he'd have come, himself. The woman sent me, bucko." He squatted beside Bannister. "She said, 'Jubal, you're the only man in the Crescent crew I can trust. I want you to help the Texan.' "

"That's the truth, Jubal?"

"I'm here, being the damn fool I am. If Matt finds out, it'll cost me my job."

"It's hard to believe."

"Don't ever let anything a woman does surprise you, bucko," Kane said. "And never wonder the why of anything one does."

Bannister lay there thinking about it, but he had difficulty concentrating and could not understand why Helen Forbes should want to help him. Things kept slipping away from him. The bearded face of Jubal Kane became blurred. He remembered vaguely how badly off Will Langley had been after being beaten. He was in worse shape.

Kane said, "Can you sit your horse, Bannister?"

"I don't know."

"We've got a long ride ahead of us."

"We?"

"Yeah. You're going with me."

"Why?"

"Harbeson may get a notion to send some of

81

the boys down this way tomorrow, to make sure you didn't get loose from your horse," Kane said. "Maybe he'll come himself. Mrs. Forbes thought of that. She gave me orders to take you to a safe place." He stood up. "I'll fetch your bronc."

Kane brought the dun, and with his help Bannister mounted. He could stay in the saddle only by taking a two-handed grip on the horn. Kane mounted his own horse, caught up the dun's reins, set out leading it. They had traveled but a short distance when Bannister's brain began to reel. He lost his hold on the pommel, and toppled from the saddle.

Kane said, "There's only one way, Bannister. I'll have to tie you on that bronc."

He got Bannister onto his feet, then onto the horse. He made a rope rigging, much like the one that had held Bannister to the dun earlier, and this held Bannister upright in the saddle, unable to fall even if he lost consciousness. Kane got back onto his sorrel and again set out leading the dun.

Bannister had no idea of how far they traveled. During much of the trip he couldn't judge time, distance or direction. He was aware that darkness overtook them, of course, and that they rode on and on through the night. Finally he saw a glimmer of lights in the distance, and was clear-minded enough at the moment to speculate upon them. He couldn't sustain curiosity about anything for long, however, and was content to let Jubal Kane take him where he would. When they at last halted, he remained slumped forward against the rope and roused only when Kane said, "Come out of it, bucko. This is the place."

He said, "What place?"

"Town called Dalton."

Bannister saw only the rear of a squat, sprawling building. It was L-shaped, and one wing of sod and the other, the newer of the two, of rough plank. Its windows showed no lights. Kane dismounted.

"Mrs. Forbes said to bring you here," he said. "These people are friends of hers. They'll look out for you."

He rapped on a door. After a minute or two lamplight bloomed behind a curtained window. Then the door opened a few inches. The old man talked to someone inside, his voice pitched low. After a lengthy discussion, the door opened wide and a young woman peered out at Bannister. She was wearing nightgown, wrapper, slippers.

She said, "I don't know about this. If my brother was here—"

"I got nowhere else to take him," Kane said.

"I know. You said that."

"He's in bad shape. He needs looking after."

"I can see that, but—"

Kane's patience ran out. He said, "Damn it, ma'am, it's a matter of life and death. If any other

Crescent hands catch him before he's himself again, he'll be a dead man. Mrs. Forbes said to bring him here, that you'd take him in."

"I don't want trouble."

"Mrs. Forbes said to pay you for your trouble."

"Oh?"

"She gave me twenty dollars. If it's not enough, you can tell her so the next time she comes to town. But it seems to me twenty is plenty."

Mention of payment put an end to the woman's objections, and after a brief debate with herself she made her decision. "All right, bring him in," she said. "I suppose he's all right, since Helen Forbes vouches for him."

Kane's reply was a disgusted grunt. He came and removed the rope from Bannister, and Bannister, with nothing to support him, again fell from the saddle.

CHAPTER EIGHT

Kane got him inside, eased him onto a chair. The room was a kitchen. A yellow-shaded lamp stood on a table covered with a red-checkered cloth. Its glare pressed against Bannister's eyes. The woman stood by the door, which she'd closed, and stared at him with horror. She was younger than he'd thought, quite a bit younger than Helen Forbes. She was darkly blonde, wholesome looking, sturdy of figure.

She said, "What happened to him?"

"He had trouble with Crescent and got the worst of it," Jubal Kane said. "Don't let his looks scare you. He wasn't bad looking before this happened. Maybe he won't be when his face heals. Get me a basin of water and I'll clean him up a little. If you've got some whiskey, fetch that too."

"There's no whiskey in this house."

"Well, make some coffee. He sure needs something." He took four five-dollar gold pieces from his pocket and laid them on the table. The girl nodded her thanks, then turned away. She brought the basin of water and a cloth for Kane, then went to the stove at the far side of the room. She fed a few sticks of kindling into the stove, filled the coffee pot and placed it on the stove. She got a cup from the cupboard and stood holding it while she watched Kane's clumsy efforts to wash Bannister's battered face clean of blood and dirt. The twenty dollars hadn't erased her displeased expression.

Kane finally called it quits and set the basin on the table. "You'll be all right here, Bannister," he said. "You're in good hands."

"Thanks, Jubal."

"Forget it."

"Thank Mrs. Forbes for me, will you?"

Kane nodded. "I'll put your horse in the barn out back." He went to the door and opened it. Then he said, "When you're able to ride, ride back to Texas. You hear?"

Bannister said, "I hear you, old man."

Kane grunted sourly, and left.

With the old man gone, the room became quiet, tautly so, except for the ticking of a clock on a shelf. The girl's silence seemed a sullen one, and he could feel her resentment of him. Well, he'd already made up his mind to leave as soon as he felt steady on his feet again. She brought him coffee, finally. He took the cup in a shaky hand. She'd been stingy with the coffee, and the brew tasted weak. But it was hot, and what he needed. He drank it quickly, and almost at once lost some of his shakiness. Taking his empty cup, the girl did not ask if he would like some more coffee, and he began forming his opinion of her. She was a thrifty sort of person, either by nature or out of necessity. Except for the money Jubal Kane had left on the table, she wouldn't have taken him in, and even now she didn't intend to let him be much of an expense to her.

He said, "You don't want me here and I don't blame you. I'll clear out, once I've caught my breath."

"You'll need to get back more than your breath."

"Still, I don't want to be a bother."

She thawed a little. "Just behave yourself, and you won't be a bother."

He looked at her with surprise, realizing only then that she might be afraid of him. He said, "The shape I'm in, I'll have to behave. What's your name?"

"Janet Maury."

"Mine's Jim Bannister. You needn't worry that I'll step out of bounds, Janet."

She nodded gravely, then turned to the stove and refilled the cup. He watched her closely, aware of how much she differed from Helen Forbes. Janet belonged to this country, being cast in the mold of pioneer women. There was strength in her, and a fine self-sufficiency. She gave him the refilled cup, then got another from the cupboard and filled it for herself. She sat at the table and studied him as she sipped coffee.

"What is your trouble with Crescent?"

"I moved a herd onto range Crescent claims."

"Others have tried that. They were wise enough to leave before they got beaten up," Janet said. "But if you're at odds with the Crescent crew, why did Helen Forbes have Jubal help you?"

"I don't know. I've been wondering about it myself."

"You don't know? That's strange."

He shrugged. "Maybe she doesn't like violence. Maybe she didn't like to see me die the way the Crescent hands planned for me. You and she are friends?"

"We're friendly, without being friends—if you know what I mean. There are so few women here in the Strip that we were drawn to each other, even though we haven't much in common. Just as my brother was drawn to John Forbes and became friendly with him."

"Your brother is a cattleman?"

"No. A merchant. He has a general store here, in the other part of the building." She smiled ruefully. "Not a very successful store. The country hasn't developed as Ben hoped when we came here two years ago. The settlers haven't come into this part of the Strip in any numbers, so he has to depend mostly on the few cattlemen for trade." She paused to drink coffee. "Ben's away tonight, visiting some of the cattlemen. They've organized into what they call the Ranchers' League. All except the Crescent outfit, of course.

They plan to elect Ben as representative to the Territorial Council from this part of the Neutral Strip."

Bannister didn't understand, and Janet saw that from his puzzled expression.

"Since you're new here, you probably don't know what's happening," she said. "The settlers are trying to organize a government. They want this country to be called Cimarron Territory, and recognized as a territory by Congress. There's to be a Territorial Council, with representatives chosen in an election. The cattlemen don't want all the representatives to be elected by the settlers. They want at least one delegate to be their man, and their choice is Ben Maury."

"But Crescent isn't backing him?"

"No. Politically, John Forbes and my brother aren't friendly at all. Mr. Forbes's company wants the Strip to remain a no man's land."

"So the outfit can have its own way here. That follows."

Janet nodded. "Crescent wants no government, or what government brings—laws, courts, homestead rights. Most of the other cattlemen are like that, too. But they know it's inevitable that we'll have a government, and they're going along with the plans so the settlers won't control the government when it's established." She gave him a probing look. "You probably won't like it, either, if you stay in the Strip."

89

"I'm staying," Bannister said. "And I'll like anything that Crescent opposes."

"Jubal gave you good advice. You'd better go back to Texas."

"There's nothing in Texas for me."

"Well, it's your life to risk," Janet said, rising. "At the moment you look as though there's not much life left in you." She got a small, unshaded lamp from the cupboard and lighted it. "You'd better get some rest. Come along. I'll show you where you can sleep."

He rose, stood swaying for a moment, then followed her from the kitchen into a hallway. In the glow of the lamp she carried, he saw that the far end of the hall led to a parlor. She turned into a small bedroom midway along it, set the lamp on the bureau, then gave the room a quick, housewifely glance to make sure everything was in order. The room was sparsely furnished, but clean and tidy.

She said, "You'll be comfortable here, I think."

"It's fine. Better than I'm used to."

"Well, good night."

"Good night, Miss Maury," he said, and stepped aside so she could leave.

She turned the lamp's wick down a trifle before leaving the room. He looked after her with a trace of amusement. Janet Maury was indeed one to save, in every small way.

The door fit improperly in the frame and its latch failed to catch, and so it remained slightly ajar when he undressed and blew out the lamp flame and got into bed. He could hear Janet moving about in the kitchen. He sighed with relief as he stretched out, but he couldn't get really comfortable even in so soft a bed. No matter in what position he lay, some part of him hurt—his ribs, his kidneys, his chest. Matt Harbeson's fists had left him with half a hundred sore spots. And the pain brought back anger, and hatred. He would even the score with Harbeson, if he accomplished nothing else in No Man's Land. On that thought, he fell asleep.

Some sound awoke him. It seemed that he'd been asleep only a few minutes, but it may have been longer, maybe as long as a couple of hours. The lamp in the kitchen still burned. He could see its yellow glow at the edge of his slightly ajar door. He heard voices, too. The girl's, and a man's. He supposed her brother had got home, and that she had waited up for him. He paid no particular attention to their voices, but without trying to eavesdrop he could overhear part of their conversation. They were discussing him, quarreling about him.

He heard Janet say, "He'll be here only a few days, and we're being well paid. It's not often twenty dollars can be earned so easily."

And her brother's reply: "What good will the

twenty dollars do us, if we have trouble with the Crescent outfit?"

"There'll be no trouble, Ben."

"You don't know Matt Harbeson like I do."

"After all, Helen Forbes sent him here," the girl said. "Harbeson can find fault with her, if he's got to find fault. Besides, the man was badly beaten up. It was the decent thing to do."

"All right," her brother said. "But see to it that he leaves before Harbeson finds out you took him in."

Bannister heard the man's angry footsteps in the hall, then the slamming of a door. A minute later the lamp went out, and he heard Janet going to her room. He lay thinking about the Maurys, without rancor. Since they feared Matt Harbeson, he could not blame them for not wanting him in their house. After all, it was foolhardy to incur the wrath of the Crescent boss—as he had found out.

He told himself that he wouldn't embarrass the Maurys with his presence for long. He would clear out in the morning, bright and early. On that decision, he rolled over and went to sleep.

It was not bright and early when he awoke, however, but midmorning.

He felt stiff and sore in numerous places, but what really bothered him was a dull, throbbing headache. He supposed that the headache came from being kicked in the head, and he wondered worriedly if some real damage had been done.

He dressed and left the room, finding that he was steadier on his legs than he'd been last night. He went to the kitchen but found no one there. The back door stood open, and he stepped out into the sunlight. From the rear of the Maury building, he could see nothing of the rest of Dalton. Nor was anyone in sight from there except a man in a wagon driving away from the town. Bannister went to the pump and started the water flowing. He ducked his head, and the chill water seemed to ease the throbbing ache. He straightened, wiped water from his face and pressed it from his hair, and then saw Janet watching him from the doorway.

"Good morning, Bannister. How are you feeling?"

"Better. No reason for me to stay longer."

"You don't look that much better."

"Still, I'll move along."

"No need to be in a hurry."

"I have a hunch there is. Your brother may not like my being here."

She smiled, her first smile in his presence. "So you heard Ben and me arguing in the middle of the night. Pay no attention to what you heard. Ben has moods. When he stays up late he's as grumpy as a bear. You stay until tomorrow, anyway, Jim. You don't look so good."

Not only the girl's manner toward him, but the girl herself seemed changed from last night, and he wondered if she too wasn't subject to moods. She wore a green skirt and a pink-and-white striped shirtwaist. Her eyes were a green-flecked gray, and a light dusting of freckles ran across her cheeks and the bridge of her nose. Smiling, she was a very attractive girl.

"Come in," she said. "I'll fix your breakfast."

He went to her. "Just a cup of coffee," he said. "It's late, and that will hold me until dinnertime." She turned her back to the door jamb, so he could move past her. He halted in the doorway, facing her. "Why the change of heart, Janet?"

"What do you mean?"

"You weren't anxious to have me here last night."

"Maybe I've decided you're not such a bad sort."

"Thanks. But I'm still a wild, red-necked Texas cattleman, and you don't have a high opinion of cattlemen."

She smiled again. "It occurred to me that if Helen Forbes is interested in you, I might be passing up something by not be interested myself. Besides, I've remembered that some cattlemen are really men of property. Are you a man of property, Jim?"

"A cold-blooded little schemer, aren't you?"

"A schemer, perhaps. But not necessarily a cold-blooded one."

"That sounds like an invitation."

"An invitation to what?"

"To find out how cold-blooded you are—or aren't," he said. Grinning broadly, he lay his hands on her shoulders. "And now is as good a time as any to find out."

She laughed and slipped away.

Later, when they were having coffee, Ben Maury came to the kitchen. He shook hands with Bannister and seemed friendly enough, when Janet introduced them. Then he said, "Sis, a customer wants to trade some eggs for enough calico to make a dress. How about you dickering with her?"

Janet nodded and went off to the store.

Maury poured coffee for himself. "I let Jan handle that sort of deal," he said. "She's better at trading than I am. A sharp one, Jan, and tight-fisted." He studied Bannister's battered face. "She didn't stretch it any. You really did take a beating."

"Yeah. And I'm obliged to you and your sister for letting me stay here last night. I was in pretty bad shape."

"Stay as long as you like. Make yourself to home."

"My being here could make trouble for you. Trouble with Matt Harbeson."

"I'm not worried about that," Maury said. "Harbeson can't run the whole Neutral Strip, no matter what he thinks."

Bannister studied him while drinking coffee. Ben Maury was a lanky man of about thirty, rather flat chested and inclined to be a bit stooped of shoulders. He had sandy hair and mustache. He was homely where his sister was handsome, and rather frail looking while she was on the sturdy side. He belonged behind a counter, Bannister decided, or at a desk. And he was, as Janet had said, a person of moods—extreme moods. Last night he'd been in a grouch. This morning he cheerfully reversed his stand about wanting Bannister gone before Harbeson learned that the Maurys were harboring him.

What had brought about that reversal, Bannister could only guess. He supposed Ben and Janet Maury had talked it over this morning and come to the conclusion that since he'd been sent there by Helen Forbes they had no reason to fear Matt Harbeson. More, Bannister had a notion that they'd decided that he was a person of some importance, because of Mrs. Forbes interest in him, and were quick to make up to anyone they believed important. It was that, or else the Maurys were a little scatterbrained.

Maury said, "What are your plans? Are you going to fight Crescent?"

"As best I can."

"How many men in your crew?"

"Only one, and he's been roughed up as bad as I am."

Maury seemed disappointed in him. "Only a one-man crew?" he said. "How many cattle you got on Crescent's range?"

"On the open range," Bannister said. "I won't admit it's Crescent's range. I've got six hundred head."

Maury nodded, looking thoughtful, and Bannister guessed that he was multiplying the current market price of cattle by six hundred. Bannister finished his coffee and started rolling a cigarette. He wondered if Maury considered him enough of a man of property to be worth cultivating.

Maury said, "You can't buck that outfit, alone. You need help."

"Yeah? And where will I get help?"

"You come along with me to the next meeting of the Ranchers' League," Maury said. "One of the reasons the League was formed is that the little cattlemen saw a need to resist Crescent. Some of the members are in the same fix as you. They founded cow camps in this part of the Strip and were moved out by Harbeson and his crew. All of them are afraid Crescent is scheming to take over most of No Man's Land." He finished his coffee, set the cup on the table and clapped Bannister on the back. "We'll talk about this again," he said heartily. "It could be that you and I can help each other. Right now, I've got to get back to the store."

He went off through the hallway, leaving

Bannister feeling that he did consider him important enough to cultivate.

When Janet returned to the kitchen, she asked, "How did you and Ben hit it off, Jim?"

"Just fine."

"You should be friends, since you're both fighting Crescent."

"Ben's fighting Crescent? That's news to me."

"Of course, he is," she said. "Not in the same way as you, perhaps. But politically. You see, the Crescent outfit is backing another man for the Territorial Council—a man not one-tenth so capable or honest as Ben. You're going to be on our side, aren't you, Jim?"

He saw that it was important to her that he be on their side. The Maurys had indeed changed their minds about him since last night. He said, "I'm with anybody who's against Crescent. But I'm not going to sit around and wait for anybody to form a government, enact laws and set up courts. I'm going to force a showdown with Harbeson and his crowd as soon as I can."

"With a gun, you mean?"

"That's the only way to handle a man like Harbeson."

"It could be you who got killed."

"That's true," he said. "But I've got to risk it. I've been driven from my ranch headquarters and my cattle. I can't let Harbeson get away with what he's done to me."

She looked at him with what seemed to be genuine concern. "Don't do anything foolhardy, Jim—please," she said. "Talk it over with Ben, and with the members of the Ranchers' League. They'll help you. I know they will. Promise?"

He regarded her with curiosity. "Why's this so important to you, Janet?"

"That's not a question I want to answer. At least, not so soon."

"I guess I know the answer."

"Well—maybe."

"I'm not much to catch any woman's eye. If I don't get the best of the Crescent crowd, I'll be flat broke. I'll have lost everything I own in the world."

Janet shook her head. "You're not going to lose your cattle," she said. "Not if you do as I ask. You will, won't you, Jim?"

He thought about it, and suddenly realized how badly off he was. He still wasn't recovered from the beating Harbeson had given him. He would be manhunted as soon as the Crescent crowd learned that he hadn't died the wretched death Harbeson had planned for him. With Will Langley laid up in a hideout camp, he had nobody siding him in his time of trouble. Having lost his guns to the Crescent riders, he couldn't even defend himself, much less regain his cattle. All in all, the only thing he could be thankful for was life itself. He gave Janet a rueful smile.

"Reckon I'll have to do as you ask," he said.

He talked it over with Ben Maury that evening, after supper, though he didn't get much said. Maury did most of the talking. A man who liked the sound of his own voice, Maury grew excited as he talked and, unable to sit still, he paced the floor. Bannister began to suspect that Ben Maury would make a better politician than a merchant.

Obviously Maury thought so too. Ambition had set him afire.

He would get himself elected to the Territorial Council, first off. Later, if he played his cards right, he might be chosen as the representative to Congress that the Council would send to Washington. Or he might wangle the appointment as territorial governor, once the United States recognized the Cimarron Territory. After all, he had the proper background. He was an educated gentleman, not a crude cattleman or a poor, dumb homesteader. The trouble was, he orated, he had so few supporters. Only the members of the Ranchers' League and the people of Dalton would vote for him against Bateman, the Crescent outfit's candidate.

"A habitual drunkard, that fellow," Maury said, scowling now as he paced to and fro.

"Why worry about him?" Bannister said. "Crescent doesn't have that many votes."

Bannister didn't understand the situation, Maury said. Crescent's candidate,—called "Judge" Bateman because he'd once been a Philadelphia lawyer—also had the backing of the Strip's lawless element. According to Maury, Bateman was a denizen of one of the settlements—Rawson Wells—inhabited solely by outlaws and the so-called sporting crowd. Rawson Wells vied with Sod Town for the dubious honor of being the Strip's toughest and most disreputable community.

If Judge Bateman were elected, Maury told Bannister, he would do his best to scuttle the plan to get the Neutral Strip recognized as a territory of the United States. The lawless element naturally wanted No Man's Land to remain an outlaw sanctuary, while the Crescent outfit, with its grandiose plan for a cattle empire, found it an advantage to keep the country in a political vacuum.

"With Bateman in the Council, they can bore from within," Maury said. "He'll belong to Crescent and the lawless element body and soul, and he's just clever enough to find a way to wreck the settlers' dream of a Cimarron Territory."

"Well, he's not elected to the Council as yet," Bannister said.

"No," Maury said. "And he never will be if I can help it."

He made a fiery little speech about his being dedicated to bringing about the defeat of Judge Bateman and foiling the machinations of the Crescent Cattle Company—a soulless corporation, as he called it—and bringing to an end the outlaws' reign of terror. Bannister found him to be a convincing orator, but he still was far less concerned with the future of No Man's Land than with his own.

He said, "According to what you told me this morning, some of the cattlemen belonging to the Ranchers' League were pushed around by Crescent. I'd like to talk to them and find out if they're planning to fight back."

"There'll be a meeting of the League Monday night," Maury told him. "I'll take you with me. But as for their fighting Crescent, I don't know. That outfit has the Indian sign on most everybody."

He went back to talking about his political campaign, and Bannister got to say no more about his feud with Crescent. Ben Maury had a one-track mind. Indeed, it seemed to Jim Bannister that the man was something of a fanatic. His monologue ended when he remembered that he had promised to see a man on business that evening. He grabbed his hat and coat and went hurrying from the house. Janet had come into the parlor a few minutes earlier, and, sitting there sewing a patch on one of Ben's shirts, she smiled wryly at Bannister.

"Ben is full of optimism tonight," she said. "Tomorrow he's likely to think he has no chance at all of being elected." She sighed. "I wish he wasn't so—so flighty."

"He's always like this?"

"Up and down. From one extreme to the other."

"I figure he'd make a good politician."

"Statesman, he calls it," Janet said. "But he was just as enthusiastic about the store when we first came here. And before that, there were other things he tried. Everything peters out for him. He's never really a failure, but he never sticks to one thing long enough to be a success, either. He loses interest too quickly." She sewed for a minute or two in silence. "This time I'm going to have something to say about it. Even if he gets elected to the Council and goes off to Beaver City, I'm going to keep the store open. Somebody has to be practical-minded."

"You think you could run the store?"

"Better than Ben does."

"But a woman in business—it seems kind of funny."

"Don't be old-fashioned, Jim. Times are changing, and some day women won't be just housewives. You'll see. I was reading in Leslie's Weekly that—"

"I don't know that I'll like women holding down men's jobs."

Janet said, "Well, I don't mean that we won't always want to be wives and mothers most of all. After all, we can't change our natures completely, and I, for one, wouldn't want to. When the right man comes along—"

Her voice trailed away, and suddenly her cheeks reddened and she lowered her gaze from his face to her sewing. And he knew then that if he wanted Janet Maury, he could certainly have her.

Once he could support a wife.

He needed to understand that. As she had said, Janet was practical-minded. She was no foolish girl to be swept off her feet and into marriage with a man who could give her no security. She would demand much of a man, and even if she did consider him a likely catch, she was also aware that his prospects at the moment were none too bright. On the other hand, she evidently banked on his will to fight to assure his future. At any rate, Bannister found it pleasant to take his ease in a comfortable room in the evening with an attractive woman for company. Indeed, it was better than anything he'd ever known and a design upon which to pattern his life.

Ben Maury didn't stay out long. He returned with news.

"Some Crescent hands just rode into town," he

said. "They're over in O'Leary's Saloon asking if anybody's seen you, Jim."

"So they've found out that I'm still alive and kicking, eh?" Bannister said. "Do they have an idea I came to Dalton?"

"No. They're just fishing."

"Is Harbeson one of them?"

"No."

"That's good," Janet said, looking straight at Bannister. "You're not ready to have a showdown with Matt Harbeson. And you know it, Jim."

Bannister looked at her with a lopsided smile, suddenly aware that Janet as a wife would not be an unmixed blessing. If the man she married gave her half a chance, she would sure try to wear the pants in the family.

Business was fairly brisk in Ben Maury's store, Saturday being the big day for the settler folks and ranchers to come to town. With Janet busy helping Ben wait on customers, Bannister loafed about the house, restlessness growing in him. Except for some slowly fading bruises, he had recovered from the beating, and inactivity made him edgy. He still kept out of sight, so no one would learn of his staying with the Maurys and report it to Crescent, and Saturday afternoon he was sitting in the kitchen, looking through some of Janet's copies of Leslie's Weekly, when

105

she came over from the store and said, "There's someone to see you, Jim."

"To see me? Now, who would that be?"

"Helen Forbes."

"Oh?"

He rose so hastily that he dropped a magazine to the floor. He picked it up, fumbling at it, and lay it on the table. He turned toward the hallway and saw a little frown of annoyance on Janet's face. The frown told him he was acting a bit too eager. He halted.

"Has something gone wrong?" he asked. "Did Harbeson find out that she sent Jubal to help me?"

"I don't think so. At least, she didn't mention that to me."

"Well, I'll see what she wants."

"Do that," Janet said. "I'll fix some tea."

He went to the parlor and found Helen Forbes sitting on the sofa. She wore gray today, a stylish suit with a flowing skirt and a form-fitting jacket with leg-of-mutton sleeves. On the white shirt-waist beneath the jacket, she wore a bit of bright green ribbon tied in a bow. He realized that he'd been wrong in thinking she wasn't beautiful. She had beauty, but it was distinctive rather than standard, wholly individual with her, and so all the more striking. She regarded him gravely.

"You've recovered," she said.

"I've had good care," he said. "Thanks to you."

106

"You needn't thank me, Bannister. I hardly expect you to."

"On the contrary, I'm indebted to you. I freed myself from my horse, but Jubal would have done it for me if I hadn't—and then I'd owe you my life, for having sent him."

"It was the humane thing to do."

"Because of you, I've found good friends in Janet and Ben."

"I was sure they'd take you in."

"It cost you twenty dollars. That at least I can repay."

"I don't want you to, Bannister."

"If you don't need the money, I'll give it to you when it's more convenient for me. How much does your husband know about your helping me, Mrs. Forbes?"

She frowned, and said sharply, "I have no secrets from my husband."

"That's as it should be. But how did he take it when you told him?"

"He thought I did the proper thing, though he didn't quite approve of my driving out to your ranch that day."

He nodded. "I can understand that," he said. "In his boots, I wouldn't approve of you going off to visit another man—even to warn him of danger."

Her frown deepened. "We always end up discussing personalities, Bannister, and that's something I disapprove of. I came here to return your guns. I had Jubal get them from your ranch headquarters. Your guns and your hat." She nodded toward the far side of the room.

He turned and saw a gunny sack lying against the wall. He looked back at her.

"I'm grateful for that too."

"I realized that unarmed you'd have no chance of escaping alive," she said. "But I'd like you to give me your promise that you won't use those guns against Crescent men unless your life is in danger."

"That's a promise I can give."

"And keep?"

"I'll keep it," he said. "If I meet up with any Crescent hands, my life will be in danger—and then I'll fight. I won't let them catch me off guard a second time."

"I should think you've had enough of fighting."

"I have."

"Then why don't you leave this country, Bannister?"

He said, "We've talked about that before, Mrs. Forbes," and then Janet came into the parlor with a tray laden with a teapot, a sugar bowl, three cups and saucers, and a dish of oatmeal cookies. He could see unconcealed curiosity in Janet's eyes, and knew that she was wondering what had been discussed during her absence in the kitchen. At the same time, a sulky expression on her face told him she was annoyed because he and Helen

Forbes had something to discuss. She'd let him know she would accept him as a suitor, and, perhaps in spite of herself, she was letting him see the possessive side of her nature. Janet would never share a man she'd marked for her own.

As Janet poured tea, Helen said, "I've been urging Bannister to leave the country, Janet. Can't you help me convince him that he should?"

"I'm sorry, Helen, but I don't see why he should."

"But surely his life is in danger."

"I realize it," Janet said, handing Helen a filled cup. "But I think Jim feels that he must risk his life. He has so much at stake."

"His cattle, you mean?"

"Of course. That many cattle are worth a small fortune."

Helen didn't reply to that, and for a little while the three of them sipped tea and munched cookies. It was a strange experience for Jim Bannister, a fantastic experience, sitting there knowing that the two women were at odds because of him. They talked polite woman-talk for a little while, ignoring him, and then Helen handed her empty cup to Janet and stood up. She thanked Janet for the tea and said she must hurry off, and Janet didn't urge her to stay longer. Bannister rose, setting his cup on the table.

He said, "Thanks again for everything, Mrs. Forbes."

"You're welcome, of course," she said. Then, studying him: "There's still no chance that you would come to terms with Crescent, is there?"

"My terms are the same as always," he told her. "I want Matt Harbeson off my neck. Nothing more, nothing less."

"Very well, Bannister."

She left then, Janet seeing her to the buckboard outside. He watched through the window. Jubal Kane had accompanied Helen to town, and he helped her to the seat. The old man climbed up and untied the reins from the whipstock. Bannister was watching them drive off when Janet returned.

She said, "She's not for you, Jim."

"Jan, you're not telling me anything I don't know."

"You're interested in her, and she's interested in you."

"That's loco. I know she's a married woman, and she thinks I'm a no-good Texas gunman, and she hates me for it."

Janet shook her head. "She's more interested in you than she has a right to be. Maybe she hates you for the trouble you've caused Crescent, but aside from that—well, she came to see you, didn't she?" She came and placed her hands on his shoulders. "A woman can never fool another woman," she said. "I don't like her doing you favors, Jim. I don't like it a little bit."

She lifted her hands to his face, touched her lips to his in a brief kiss. Before he could respond, she slipped away to the door opening into the store. She smiled at him from there, her lips curving ripely.

"I can be as brazen as she, if I have to be," she said, and then the door closed behind her.

Bannister stood there badly confused. He had Janet's kiss on his lips, and Helen on his mind.

CHAPTER NINE

Monday evening Bannister came out of hiding.

He rode from Dalton with Ben Maury, heading east along the road that led to Beaver City, and it was good to be in the saddle again. Loafing around, even in comfort and with attractive feminine company, wasn't for him. At least, not in large doses. He needed to be on the move, to be up and doing. There was a drive in him that couldn't be ignored.

He experienced an occasional dull headache, a lingering reminder of that kick to the head, but otherwise he had recovered from the roughing-up. He felt fit enough to buck Crescent again, and the time had come to plan his next move.

Unlike Ben and Janet, he had no hope that the members of the Ranchers' League would side him in his feud with Crescent. But some of them might have ideas about how to fight Matt Harbeson and his crew. Harbeson must have a weak spot somewhere, and any information revealing it would be useful. Besides, Bannister had his curiosity about the Ranchers' League, and he felt that no harm and perhaps a little good would come of his meeting its members.

They'd set out from Dalton at dusk, traveling at a brisk pace, and about two hours after nightfall they came to a couple of buildings at a crossroads. The main building was squat, sprawling and sod-walled. A roofed gallery ran across its front, and a crudely lettered sign over the entrance bore the legend: *Hanlon's Place.* Its doorway and windows were bright with lamplight. A dozen or more saddle horses stood about, half of them at a hitch-rack and the others loose with trailing reins. As Maury and Bannister dismounted, two other riders loomed out of the darkness, coming in from the north. One of the pair was a craggy-faced, gray-mustached old-timer, the other a lank, dour-faced man of middle age.

Maury affected the hearty manner of a politician in greeting them, saying loudly, "Good evening, gentlemen. How are you, Jess? How's the missus, Clay?"

The older man merely grunted, and the other said, grudgingly, "The missus is all right."

Ben Maury seemed not to notice that they lacked his enthusiasm, and after they dismounted he introduced Jim Bannister. The old man was Jess Tolliver, the younger, Clay Roland. While Maury explained that each of them owned a one-man cow outfit and both had been pushed around by Crescent, they stood there sizing up Bannister with more friendliness than they'd shown Maury.

"We've been hearing about you," Tolliver told Bannister.

"About me?"

"About your trouble with Crescent."

"News gets around in this country."

"If it's news about Crescent, it does," Tolliver said. "The story is that Matt Harbeson chased you off without your stock. Any truth to that?"

"My cattle are still at Boot Creek," Bannister said. "I'll be going back there."

Both cattlemen stared at him. Tolliver said, "You will, eh?" and then Ben Maury said, "Let's go in and get the meeting started."

The main room of Hanlon's Place contained a crude plank bar and several tables. Opening off from it was a smaller room stocked with merchandise, a none too prosperous appearing store. Four men sat at a table, and eight others had lined up at the bar. All were cow country men, all typical of the breed, though Bannister judged their ages ran from the low twenties to the late sixties. The bartender was Hanlon, a very bald and enormously fat man. Bannister saw two house women, one a faded blonde and the other a slip of a girl with hennaed hair; and also, sitting alone at a corner table, at a game of solitaire, a pale lean man wearing a black suit, a flowered vest, a white shirt with a string tie. The card player had a spell of coughing as Bannister's gaze found him. He coughed into a handkerchief, and a red spot appeared in each of his sickly white cheeks with the effort of controlling the spell. This consumptive tinhorn completed the picture of Hanlon's Place—whiskey, women, gambling.

The roadhouse wouldn't get much homesteader trade, Bannister knew, settlers being mostly family men. The place would have to depend upon the cattlemen and others cast in the same hardy mold who liked their pleasures raw and rowdy. He wondered if Ben Maury was foolish enough to think that the likes of Hanlon and the gambler would support him in his political campaign.

Maury took Bannister around and introduced him to the other cattlemen. It was apparent that they'd all heard of his feud with the Crescent outfit, and also that his stock rated higher with them than Maury's. The merchant-turned-politician did not hold the respect of these men. Basically, they were no more anxious than the Crescent people to have No Man's Land made an organized territory, and Bannister sensed that if they could find another way to hamstring that outfit, they would give Maury no support at all. Half a dozen more men arrived within the next few minutes, and finally Maury called the meeting to order.

He did his best to turn it into a political rally, and he made a laudable speech about the benefits to be derived from having the Neutral Strip organized into the Cimarron Territory and recognized by Congress. Mostly, he spoke of the danger of allowing the Crescent Cattle Company and the outlaws and the sporting crowd to elect Judge Bateman to the Council. He pointed with pride to his own qualifications and viewed with alarm Bateman's subservience to the men who wanted the Strip to remain one vast outlaw hangout—and an empire for the Crescent Cattle Company. He never touched on his own desire to see the country become a haven for homesteaders, because dirt farmers would put grassland to the plow, and offer still another threat to these small ranchers.

He finished up in half an hour, exhorting them to round up voters for him in the coming elections. He was a fiery speaker, but Bannister had the feeling that he failed to convince the members of the Ranchers' League.

Maury had his axe to grind. He wanted to see himself in public office and to bring in great numbers of settlers. But the cattlemen also had an axe to grind.

The meeting turned into an open forum after Maury's speech, and several ranchers, one after the other, took the floor and said their pieces. All in all, it boiled down to the proposition that none of the cattlemen wanted to be crowded out by homesteaders—and they wanted some assurance from Ben Maury that a fair portion of the Strip would remain cattle range.

There were three factions among the cattlemen, it seemed. Originally, they had banded together in the League to act against the rustlers and horse thieves. The men most concerned about the outlaws wanted law and courts in the Strip, and dour-faced Clay Roland acted as their spokesman. The second group, headed by old Jess Tolliver, feared and hated the Crescent outfit and hoped that an organized government would halt its plan for controlling too much of the Strip's graze. The third group—half a dozen fence-straddlers—didn't know whether they wanted the country to be organized or not. A lot of argument developed, and Jim Bannister found it pretty dull. Finally, the debate came to a head with a vote on whether or not the League should support Ben Maury for the Council or to keep out of politics. A small majority gave it to Maury, and the meeting was adjourned.

Soon afterward, Clay Roland and one other man took their leave. Being married, they had reason to get home. Three men got into a poker game with the sickly house gambler, and a couple of others paired off with the women. The remainder lingered to drink and talk, Ben Maury circulating among them and talking about the coming election. Old Jess Tolliver sought out Bannister at a table, and they shared a bottle.

Tolliver said, "So you're going back to Boot Creek, friend?"

"That's right."

"To get run off again?"

"Crescent didn't exactly run me off the first time," Bannister said. "A bunch of Crescent hands jumped me, caught me off guard. They gave me a beating and tied me on my horse and headed it through empty country with its reins tied back. Matt Harbeson figured that would be the end of me. But I got loose, and now I'm going back."

"Next time he'll make sure of you."

"He won't get another chance."

"Don't be too sure. Matt Harbeson is as smart as he is tough."

"I know what he is," Bannister said sourly. "A damn hard man to beat. He's *muy hombre.* But he must have a weak spot, a blind side."

"I've never noticed it," Tolliver said. "I don't think you've got as much chance of getting the best of him as a snowball has of freezing hell over. I wish you could, though. I'd like to see Harbeson and the whole Crescent outfit take a licking. I was in the Strip before Crescent came into the country. I figured I'd located in a place where I could stay put the rest of my days. Harbeson decided otherwise. And when they jumped me, him and his gunhands killed my son."

Tolliver reached for the bottle. He poured and downed a quick drink.

A man named Rumans called from the bar, "Hey, Bannister, is your brand the J-Bar-B?"

Bannister nodded. "It is. Why do you ask?"

Rumans gestured toward a companion. "Mario says on his way here this afternoon, when he was cutting across Crescent range, he saw a big herd of J-Bar-B cattle being driven toward the Kansas line by a bunch of hardcases from Rawson Wells."

For a moment Bannister sat stunned by the news. Then he rose and faced the man called Mario. "Why the hell didn't you tell me about this before now?"

Mario Dunn was half Mexican, half Irish, a lean, handsome man whose pale blue eyes seemed misplaced in his dusky face. He shrugged. "I didn't think the J-Bar-B was your brand until Al here said it might be."

"You're sure of the brand?"

"I'm sure. I figured Crescent was trailing cattle to the railroad, or that it was a Texas outfit passing through. Then I got close enough to see the J-Bar-B brand. By that time a couple of the trail hands came riding at me. One was Jake Maugher, so I knew it was a rustler crowd with a steal—and I got out of there pronto."

"Jake Maugher?"

"Yeah. You know him?"

"I know him," Bannister said. "Where'd you see the herd?"

"About three miles north of Crescent head-quarters," Mario Dunn said. "If Maugher bedded the herd down tonight, it would be at Drum Creek—about three miles north of where I saw it. If he's keeping on the move, he'll likely make the Kansas line by morning."

Bannister said, "Thanks for the information," and headed for the door.

Old Tolliver called after him, "Hell, man, you're not going after that crowd alone, are you?"

Bannister faced about in the doorway. It was tautly quiet in the barroom now. Everyone, including even the two floozies, was staring at him. He looked at Jess Tolliver, then let his gaze go from one to another of the cattlemen. Ben Maury said, "Jess is right, Jim. You can't buck that crowd alone."

"Do I hear an offer of help?"

Jess Tolliver stood up. "We'll side you," he said. "That's the purpose of the Ranchers' League, to put a stop to the rustling here in No Man's Land."

"Better go easy," Mario Dunn said. "You don't know what you're letting yourself in for, Jess."

"What's that mean, Mario?"

"Those Rawson Wells hombres ain't in this alone," Dunn said. "Matt Harbeson and half a dozen of his riders were out there watching the rustlers trail that herd across Crescent range. Sure as shooting, Harbeson's in cahoots with Jake Maugher on this deal, and if we ride with Bannister were sure to have trouble with Crescent. Me, I'm not anxious for that kind of trouble."

Tolliver muttered, "Yeah, that's a horse of another color." Avoiding Bannister's gaze, he sank heavily onto his chair and again reached for the bottle of whiskey on the table.

Bannister again looked from face to face, and now none of them would look back at him.

Ben Maury said, "Jim, you'll have to take the loss. It'd be suicide for you to go out there. After all, your life is worth more than those cattle."

Bannister said, "This is hard to believe—that Matt Harbeson has the Indian sign on all of you." His voice was heavy with disgust but it brought no reply. "To hell with the lot of you!" he said.

He went out to his horse, and he rode away from Hanlon's Place.

CHAPTER TEN

It was a black night, with few stars and the moon smudged over by clouds. Bannister rode at a hard lope for a time, until he realized, through his rage, that he would be wise not to tire his mount. He might need it fresh, later on. He slowed to a walk, alternating it with an easy lope.

His anger didn't lessen, but he brought it under control. And so, more calm in his mind, he admitted that he shouldn't blame those men back in Hanlon's Place. It was one thing to fight rustlers, another to feud with an outfit like Crescent. Rustlers were dangerous only when cornered, and would run more often than not before a trap could be sprung. But Crescent would never run, or even back down in the slightest degree. Men like Matt Harbeson and his tough hands needed no urging to go on the prod, and so they were always dangerous.

After all, the members of the Ranchers' League were only raggedy-pants cowmen. Few of them kept hired hands, and those few would hardly have gunmen on their payroll. They lived isolated from each other, and that made them individual sitting ducks for an enemy like Crescent. Only if they stayed neutral would Crescent remain an inactive enemy. No, Bannister couldn't blame them for deciding not to side him.

Naturally they considered him foolhardy to be riding alone against the rustlers. Rustlers would put up a fight when they had a chance to win, and in this case, with Jake Maugher hating his guts, they would welcome a fight. He had no idea of the odds against him, but they would surely be great. Still, he would have the advantage of surprise. He intended to use stealth against them, and he shouldn't encounter any Crescent riders. It didn't seem likely that Harbeson would spend the night with the rustler crowd . . . unless he suspected that Bannister might show up. But no. It wouldn't occur to Harbeson that he knew they were being driven out of No Man's Land.

Bannister had a cattleman's hatred of rustlers, but he directed his rage at Matt Harbeson rather than at Jake Maugher. The rustlers wouldn't have dared operate on range claimed by Crescent without Harbeson's permission. It followed that the idea of making off with the J-Bar-B cattle was Harbeson's. It had been Harbeson's logical next move, Bannister reflected, and it killed two birds with one stone, so to speak. It rid the range of the J-Bar-B herd and, if successful, it would ruin the herd's owner. Bannister had to admit that old Jess Tolliver had been right in saying that Matt Harbeson was as smart as he was tough.

He came finally to a shallow stream and

supposed it was Drum Creek. He reined in to rest his horse and to listen for sounds in the darkness. He heard a coyote howl mournfully far in the distance, but nothing more. After about ten minutes, he forded the creek and rode along its north bank. He held the dun to a slow walk. The thick, high grass muffled the striking of the horse's hoofs against the ground. The only sounds were the creaking of saddle leather and the occasional rattle of bit chain. After another mile, Bannister began to think that the rustlers hadn't bedded down the herd, but meant to keep it on the trail to Kansas throughout the night.

Then he saw the yellow-red glow of a campfire.

He pulled up short, peering toward the flickering light. Somebody had camped close to the creek, on this side of it. He could see a small bunch of saddled horses, standing droopingly with trailing reins, just beyond the fire, and the tarp-wrapped figures of half a dozen men. He knew that he'd found the rustlers. They had their horses saddled, ready to ride in case the herd spooked or somebody showed up to dispute their ownership of it. He peered into the darkness and made out the dark mass of bedded-down cattle with two men riding night herd. He considered a moment, making his decision. Then he turned back a short distance and rode to get north of the herd without being seen or heard by the two nighthawks. Ten minutes later, he reached a position a hundred yards north of the cattle and again reined in.

Alone against so many, he had but one course open to him. It wasn't one he liked. He'd have to stampede the herd, and like any real cowman he hated to spook cattle. Still, he wanted the herd out of the rustlers' possession and back across the creek, as far back onto the range claimed by Crescent as he could get them, and he was in too ugly a humor to care how he managed it. He eased his revolver from its holster.

He hesitated a moment, well aware of the danger. But his resolve not to be defeated by Matt Harbeson was greater than the fear that came to him, and the moment of doubt passed. He kneed the dun into motion and rode directly toward the herd. He was quite close when one of the night herders spotted him.

"Sparky, somebody's prowling out there!"

He didn't hear the other man's reply. He jabbed spurs to the dun, gave a yell to start it off, and fired three shots into the air as fast as he could work the Colt's hammer and trigger.

The night quiet was completely shattered as the mass of longhorns lurched onto their feet, bellowing in common panic. With a thunderous pounding of hoofs and clashing of horns, six hundred head of fear-crazed Texas cattle broke into a wild stampede. One of the night herders screamed as he came near to being run down.

Then, escaping the hurtling mass of cattle, he continued in panicky flight until darkness swallowed him. The other man had been in no danger at all, and now he opened fire on Bannister. The muzzle flashes of his gun made him an easy target, and Bannister, riding in the direction the herd had taken, aimed a shot that tore the man from the saddle.

Ahead, the rustlers at the camp had a brief moment in which to leap from their beds and onto their mounts. One was a little too slow. His scream rang out above the bellowing of the frenzied cattle, and then cut off as the dense wave of maddened beasts engulfed him. The others rode for their lives, ahead of the stampede and gradually swerving out of its path. One man's mount spooked and went into a wild bucking, and the leaders of the herd caught him. Horse and man went down, and the bulk of the herd surged over them. The riders who escaped were lost to Bannister in the darkness, and then the cattle began racing across the creek. A gun cut loose at him, and even above the din he heard the shriek of the slug.

He answered the shot, firing twice, and had a glimpse of a rider swerving away and reeling in the saddle. His horse hit the creek and went splashing across at a gallop. A gun cracked behind Bannister, and he twisted in the saddle and saw two shadowy figures fording the creek.

He drew a bead on one, squeezed the trigger. The Colt failed to go off, and he knew that he'd already fired its last cartridge. He holstered it, tied a knot in the dun's reins and jerked his rifle from its boot. Another shot sounded behind him.

He was following the stampeding herd, but it continued to run at express train speed, drawing away from him. He shot a glance over his shoulder and saw that he had lengthened his lead and was now out of hand gun range. He began to fear that he would run the dun into the ground, so he took hold of the reins and slowed it to an easy lope. He continued at that pace for perhaps a quarter of a mile, and then another backward look showed him that one of his pursuers had quit the chase. The other came on doggedly.

This would be a man with hate in his soul, not one merely bent on recovering stolen stock. Something greater than greed motivated this rider, so he must be Jake Maugher. Bannister thought: Call it quits, you fool! He'd accomplished his mission. He was sick of shooting men, even though they were rustlers. He didn't want to kill Jake Maugher.

He traveled another mile, losing some of his lead and feeling the dun's sides pumping like over-worked bellows against his legs. The horse had had too much taken out of it by that first long, hard gallop, and if he didn't give it a rest, he would almost certainly kill it. He waited no longer, but jerked it to a rearing halt and flung himself from the saddle. The oncoming rider had anticipated such a move and instantly reined in and opened fire. The slug passed so close that Bannister flinched. Jerking the Winchester to his shoulder, Bannister drove a quick shot at Maugher. It missed the rustler, but creased his horse. The animal shrieked, began a wild bucking. Shouting an oath, Maugher dropped from its back. He swung his gun up to bead Bannister, but then, as had happened to Bannister earlier, its hammer fell on an already fired cartridge.

Like a man gone berserk, Maugher yelped with frustration and flung the empty weapon with all his might. Bannister ducked it, then leaped forward to keep the rustler from getting the rifle off his saddle. Maugher reached the horse an instant before him and jerked the rifle from its scabbard. He worked the lever as he whipped around, but Bannister, sick of such a bloody game and reluctant to shoot, clubbed at Maugher. The Winchester's stock caught the rustler alongside the head, knocking him to the ground.

Maugher lay stunned, unable to resist when Bannister took his rifle. He lay there staring up at Bannister, and despite the darkness Bannister could see the wicked gleam of hatred in his eyes.

"Damn you, Bannister!" he gasped. "Damn you to hell!"

Bannister took a backward step and threw the captured rifle from him. He stood listening for other riders but heard none. He could hear the herd, far off.

Maugher continued to curse him, in a low savage voice.

Bannister said, "Jake, with the pressure of one finger I can kill you. Are you such a fool that you don't understand that?"

Caution came to Jake Maugher. He struggled to his feet.

Bannister said, "I killed your brother to save myself, not because I wanted him dead, and you know it. I'm letting you live because I'm not anxious to have you on my conscience. Give this some thought. Maybe it'll bring you to your senses. You—" He broke off, knowing it was useless. Jake Maugher would hate him and want revenge until one or the other died. Gesturing with his rifle, he said, "Get on your horse and ride out, Jake."

Maugher had trouble mounting. He was still shaky and his horse still spooked and acted up. But finally he gained the saddle, and sat staring down at Bannister. He said nothing. He didn't have to. His eyes spoke more viciously than words. Then at last he wheeled his horse about and headed back toward Drum Creek.

Bannister waited until the rustler disappeared in the darkness, then went to his horse. He didn't mount, but led the still heaving dun. He saw nothing of his herd, and no longer heard the sound of the stampede. The cattle had run far. Maybe they were still running, and that was how he wanted it. By tomorrow they would be widely scattered and difficult to gather. But he doubted that Jake Maugher and the survivors of his band would make another attempt to steal his J-Bar-B herd in the near future. From here on out he'd have Matt Harbeson and his crew to buck, and they wouldn't be as easy to deal with as the Maugher crowd.

After several miles afoot, he mounted and rode on, trying to figure out where to strike next.

At midmorning Matt Harbeson rode in off the range and found Jake Maugher at Crescent headquarters. The rustler was making himself at home. He'd off-saddled his gray horse and now had a feedbag on it which he'd borrowed, along with some grain, from the barn. Maugher was hunkered down in the shade of the building, a cigarette drooping from his lips and a murky look in his eyes.

Harbeson reined in before him. "What the hell you doing here?"

"Waiting to see you."

"See me about what? Something go wrong?"

"Everything went wrong."

"Bannister?"

"Yeah, Bannister," Maugher said savagely. He told what had happened last night, his voice harsh with his vile humor. "Two of the boys are dead, and one has a bullet hole through his guts. And you ask if something went wrong!"

"Eight of you, and one of him," Harbeson said. "What are you, a bunch of—"

"He's tricky as the Devil himself, I tell you."

"Yeah. How'd he find out you were moving his herd?"

"How should I know?"

Harbeson swore. "I should have put a bullet in him that day at Boot Creek."

"Well, why didn't you?" Maugher said.

Harbeson scowled, but said nothing. He did answer the question in his own mind, however. He hadn't wanted Helen Forbes to witness the Texan's death and hold it against him. He'd known that she already considered him a brute, and the knowledge had bothered him. For her benefit, he'd given Sanchez and Buck orders to start Bannister back toward Texas, and to free him from his bonds once they had him well on his way. Out of her hearing, he'd told them to let him remain tied and to turn his horse loose out in the badlands. It hadn't worked, but the woman's opinion of him was important. Ever since the day of her arrival at Crescent Ranch, he'd wanted her. Sooner or later she'd get over looking at him as if he'd crawled out from under a rock. Sooner or later she'd realize two things: one, that he was far more of a man than her husband; and two, that a man needed to be hard—brutal, if she insisted—to survive and make something of himself in this country.

Jake Maugher said, "Because of you, Matt, I had a lot of grief for nothing. I don't aim to come off with the short end. What are you going to do about it?"

"Nothing."

"What do you mean, nothing? Stealing that herd was your idea. Me and the boys were doing you a favor. We figure you owe us something."

"Why, you poor fool, you had a chance to make yourself a bigger stake than you ever dreamed of," Harbeson said. "That herd would have brought you a fortune. You let the chance slip through your fingers. Blame yourself, not me."

Maugher looked up at him in that wicked way again. "You'd better think it over, friend," he said. "If Bannister ever finds out you put us up to stealing his herd—"

"Tell him and be damned," Harbeson said. "He's already figured that out, anyway."

He wheeled his horse away, heading toward the cookshack for a cup of coffee. As he dismounted he saw Dick Mercer come from the main house. So Mercer had got back from Kansas. Nice little messenger boy, Mercer. Bannister threw a scare into Forbes, and the dude sent Mercer all the way to Kansas to put a yell for help on the telegraph. Forbes had told Mercer to hang around until he got a reply from Philadelphia, so . . . Damn the kid.

Mercer came across the yard, rolling a smoke on the way.

He said, "Matt, Mr. Forbes wants to see you."

Harbeson said, "Had yourself a holiday, did you?"

"Sort of. But I only did as I was told."

"Next time you do as Forbes tells you, bucko, you're out of a job."

Mercer looked startled. "You mean I did something wrong? I didn't know—"

"You know now," Harbeson said, and headed for the house.

He was in such an ugly mood that he didn't even notice Helen Forbes dusting furniture in the parlor. He strode across the hall, and into Forbes's study. He knew that the reply to the ranch manager's telegram would be bad news for him, and that, on top of Bannister's latest whingding, made him mad enough to bite nails. He found Forbes seated at his desk.

"All right," he said, "let's have it."

Forbes handed him a paper. "This is addressed to you as well as me, Matt."

Harbeson's first impulse was to crumple the paper into a ball and throw it back at Forbes, unread. Curiosity got the better of him, however, and he stared at the precise handwriting of the telegrapher who had received the message. He read:

PLANNING VISIT CRESCENT RANCH.
ENTRAINING TODAY. MEANWHILE,
INSTRUCT YOU HALT ALL ACTIVITIES
AGAINST SQUATTERS. J. P. VORHEES.

Harbeson dropped the paper onto the desk. "Forbes, you've pulled a fool stunt in bringing that old man out here."

For once his voice lacked bluster. Vorhees was the one company bigwig who would disapprove of his operation of the outfit, and this news had hit him hard enough to knock the fury out of him. In fact, it threw a scare into him. He knew that the other company officers—the ones who until now had given him a free hand here—feared the old man. Vorhees's word was law within the Crescent Cattle Company and any decision he handed down would stick. He began to fear that he might lose his job when the old man learned the whole truth of the situation here. It was a nightmarish fear.

Forbes said, "I feel that it was a wise move, Matt," and he actually sounded firm, armed as he was with the knowledge of Vorhees's coming visit. "Things have got out of hand here, and someone in authority should know it."

"Old Vorhees will ruin this ranch."

"I doubt that."

"He doesn't know a damn thing about operating a cow outfit."

Forbes said, "You'll get a hearing, Matt. Mr. Vorhees is a fair person. He'll listen to your side of the story, and if you can justify your actions— well, all the more power to you."

Harbeson knew that he could never make the old man swallow much of what he had pulled, and he knew that Forbes knew it. He said, "And if I can't make him agree that I'm right?"

Forbes shrugged. "That's for you to worry about," he said. "By the way, I want to drive to Dalton today. Have one of the hands hitch up the buckboard, will you?"

Harbeson gave him a final scowl and strode out of the study. Helen Forbes came from the parlor with a feather duster in her hand, and this time he noticed her with a sharp awareness. She looked directly at him, and through him. It was as though she looked into him and found nothing worthwhile, and suddenly he hated her. He slammed the front door as he left the house. He thought: Damn you, I'd like to show you a thing or two! And then the idea leaked into his mind. He would show her, all right. The way to show her, the idea had been born fully formed and foolproof.

He halted on the porch, taking out makings and building a smoke, going over the idea and building it into a plan. He needed to convince

J. P. Vorhees that the squatters were making the trouble, feuding against Crescent, and he was merely trying to protect the ranch. He needed to rid himself of Jim Bannister, and he would be better off rid of John Forbes, because the dude would be the one witness against him when Vorhees arrived. Bannister had threatened Forbes, and Forbes was going to Dalton. If somebody shot him dead on the way, Bannister could be blamed. And with Bannister wanted for murder, dead or alive, with a fat reward offered to speed things up, every man in the Strip who could ride a horse and pack a gun, would try to collect. And that would finish Bannister.

Harbeson lighted his cigarette, dragged hard on it. He smiled over the plan. He liked it more and more, considering that John Forbes would be leaving a widow.

He saw Dick Mercer come from the cookshack. He went down the porch steps and called to the cowpuncher.

"Dick, hitch up the grays to the buckboard," he said. His tone was almost civil. "Forbes wants to drive to town."

He headed toward the barn, where Jake Maugher waited, chewing on a stem of straw, his expression still mean.

"What about it, Matt?"

"A deal, Jake."

Maugher stayed hunkered down with his back

136

to the barn well, but his eyes showed surprise. "What kind of a deal?"

"Those J-Bar-B cattle are scattered to hell and gone across Crescent range. Right?"

"Yeah."

"Gather them in small bunches," Harbeson said. "Forty, fifty head at a shot. Take them to Kansas and sell them. Hire a couple of riders to help. I'll give you the money to pay them. I get back half what you collect for the cattle."

"So now you're cutting yourself in, are you?"

"Those cows are on Crescent range. I'm handing them over to you."

"You think. You're forgetting Bannister."

Harbeson grinned. "You can forget him, too," he said. "He'll be taken care of." He dug some money from his pocket and handed it to Maugher. "Start gathering the cattle within the next two, three days. And listen, bucko—don't try to cross me up."

He went to his horse and stepped to the saddle. As he rode from the yard, he saw Dick Mercer bringing the buckboard team in from the fenced meadow north of headquarters.

He headed south at an easy lope for a couple of miles, and then, upon sighting four Crescent punchers some distance ahead, he abruptly turned east. He aimed in the direction of Dalton, coming at high noon to a broad rock field known among the crew as the Graveyard. There was a jumble of huge boulders and giant rock slabs, many piled one atop the other, and Harbeson found his way in among them. He paused briefly to study his back trail. Seeing nothing other than a few grazing cattle, he rode on through the rocks until he came close to the north edge of the field. He dismounted, took his rifle from its boot and went on afoot. He climbed to a height of about a hundred feet, where the rocks were pyramided, and from this vantage place, well hidden, he had a view of a wide portion of the range and of the road which passed the field at a point only a hundred yards away. At the moment nothing moved along the road, and Harbeson, leaning his rifle against a rock, rolled and lighted a cigarette.

After a while the buckboard and team appeared on the road, approaching from the direction of Crescent headquarters. Harbeson dropped the half-smoked cigarette and reached for his rifle. He levered a cartridge into the firing chamber and leveled the barrel across a flat rock formation. The team approached at a fast trot, and Harbeson saw that Forbes was alone. He'd had a small nagging fear that Helen might have decided to postpone her housework and accompany her husband. He might not have been able to go through with it if Helen had been with Forbes.

In a few minutes, he heard the rhythmic drumming of the grays' hoofs and the creak of wheels. He crouched there, behind the rock, and beaded the man. He followed Forbes with the Winchester's sights. The buckboard passed directly below him, and in the next moment he was aiming at Forbes's back.

Still he hesitated, puzzled by his own reluctance to squeeze the trigger.

With his resolve wavering, he reminded himself that his whole future was at stake. Crescent Ranch was more than a job to him; it was his life. He already had a sizable stake in it, and he'd have a bigger one with the passing years. Cut loose from Crescent, he'd be lost. All that was important to him was in jeopardy because of Forbes—and Bannister. He needed to be rid of them both.

He muttered, "Now!" and squeezed the trigger.

The crack of the shot was still roaring in his ears when John Forbes jerked violently, half rose from the seat, then fell loosely from the buckboard. The team spooked and, with no hands on the reins, broke into a gallop. Forbes sprawled at the edge of the road, face down and unmoving.

Harbeson stared at his victim for several long minutes, his heavy face expressionless except for a slight frown that suggested some uncertainty about the wisdom of what he'd done. Finally, with a shrug, he turned to go to his horse. And then, glancing west along the road, he saw that a rider had been following the buckboard at a distance of about half a mile. The rider had stopped upon hearing the rifle shot, and now he wheeled his horse about and headed back toward Crescent headquarters.

For a moment fear chilled Matt Harbeson. Then, reason returned. Whoever the rider was—a Crescent hand, Jake Maugher, or some stranger—he could not have recognized anybody at that distance. He got hold of himself. He climbed down from the rocks, mounted his horse, and set out on a wide swing about the range—as a ranch foreman had a right to do.

CHAPTER ELEVEN

Coming into Dalton at midmorning, Jim Bannister made no attempt to avoid being seen by the inhabitants of the grubby town. His encounter with the Maugher crowd last night had proved that he was fit again, as ready as he would ever be for a showdown with Crescent. He would hide no longer.

He swung around to the rear of the Maurys' building, and Janet appeared at the kitchen door as he dismounted. Her face lighted at sight of him, and when he went to her, she took hold of his hands.

"Jim, I've been so worried."

"I wasn't in much danger."

"When Ben came home and you weren't with him—"

She left the rest unspoken, but drew him inside. His reaction was automatic. He caught her about the waist, held her tightly against him, and kissed her with a fervor that surprised him. At the moment he felt sure he was in love with Janet Maury. But the next moment, she held herself from him.

"You got back your cattle, Jim?"

"Yes."

"Well, that's the important thing."

He said, "Yes, that's the important thing," and the spell broke. He felt cheated. It occurred to him that a woman could be a bit too practical-minded. Releasing her, he said, "At least, I got them away from the rustlers. They're scattered over half of No Man's Land."

"Ben and I have been talking it over," she said, unaware of his withdrawal. "It seems so foolish for you to go on fighting Crescent. The sensible thing is to find another range. Don't you agree?"

"I should agree, I suppose," he said. "But I've made up my mind not to be driven off Boot Creek range. Besides, right now my cattle are in the middle of range Crescent claims and I doubt if Matt Harbeson would let me gather them without a fight. And I've got no crew to help me gather them, anyway."

"Couldn't you hire a few men?"

"They'd have to be gunmen, Jan, and I haven't the money to hire such hands."

"Maybe the Ranchers' League would help round up your cattle."

He shook his head. "That crowd won't make a move against Crescent. Matt Harbeson has the Indian sign on them. I found that out last night."

Janet frowned in thought. "It doesn't seem possible that Matt Harbeson would keep you from gathering your cattle if he knew you wanted to move off Crescent range. Suppose Ben goes out there and has a talk with him?"

"It'd do no good, Jan. Harbeson wants me either dead or ruined."

"You could be wrong about him."

"No."

She was suddenly angry. "Jim, I think you're being stubborn—as stubborn as you make out Matt Harbeson to be. You won't give an inch. You won't try to settle this trouble sensibly. You're not showing good judgment in keeping this feud going. It's all a matter of foolish pride with you, this wanting to stay at Boot Creek."

She seemed a stranger now, not the girl he had taken in his arms and thought he loved. She just plain didn't understand him. He said, "Jan, I guess we'd better quit talking about it. We'll quarrel if we keep on discussing it."

"I'm afraid we will, Jim."

"A man has got to do what he thinks is right for him."

"When you discover how wrong you are, it may be too late."

"That could be," he said. "Anyway, I'll be on my way. Thanks for everything, Jan. Say good-bye to Ben for me, eh?"

He turned to the door.

Janet said, "Don't go angry, Jim—please."

He faced her, and smiled. "I can't be angry with you."

She came to him and slipped her arms about his neck. "I'm glad you can't," she said. Her body

143

strained against his. "I'm trying to reason with you only because I want you to be safe. I don't want you to lose your life or your cattle. Won't you keep both safe, darling—for me? Won't you think things over and try to see that I'm asking only what's best for you?"

He said, "I'll give it some thought, of course."

He kissed her, but then, riding out a few minutes later, he realized how little there had been in the meeting of their lips. A kiss from Janet was a cool, calculating thing, a caress meant to bind him to her and her way of thinking. He didn't doubt that she was fond of him, but her fondness was tempered by her knowledge of his potential worth, and it would die if he lost the cattle which were his stake in the future. If Janet Maury had any deep well of passion for a man to plumb, she kept it hidden. He felt a need for her, now, but a girl who had a tally-book for a mind and a till for a heart would put up an awful lot of resistance before she settled for love, with no thought of any other reward from her man. Would Janet ever be capable of that? Maybe. He'd have to see.

Bannister followed the south road out of Dalton until it came to a dead-end in a section taken over by homesteaders. After passing their grubby places and tilled fields, he turned westward and at midafternoon reached the sand flats. He swung southwest now, all this while seeing no other riders. At sundown he reached the range of low hills in which he'd set up the camp for Will Langley, and in the hazy dusk he came to the camp site at the base of a craggy cliff from which a spring flowed and formed a little pool.

Langley was gone, and so were his mount and the pack-horse. The ashes of a fire remained, and also a little brush kindling. The camp gear and store of provisions were in a cache among some boulders. Dismounting, Bannister decided that Langley must have recovered. But where had the man gone?

He off-saddled his dun, started a fire and cooked his evening meal. Night fell by the time he'd eaten, so he got his bedroll from the cache and turned in. He felt a little disturbed over Langley's leaving.

It seemed unlikely that Langley had headed back to Texas. He'd promised to see things through, and that stubborn streak of his would certainly keep him in No Man's Land until he either paid Crescent back for the lashing he'd received, or died trying. It occurred to Bannister that Langley had gone out searching for him, and if that were the case, he would sooner or later return to the hideout. On that thought, Bannister slept.

He loafed about the camp all the next day, and when Langley didn't show up by sundown, he saddled the dun and rode down from the hills.

145

He'd convinced himself that Langley had run into trouble with Crescent, and he meant to find out just what had happened. Nightfall came as he crossed the grassland to the north of the hills, and within a mile of Boot Creek he saw a gleam of lamplight at his building.

He rode slowly toward his headquarters, hoping he'd find Langley there. He reached the creek, dismounted in a brush thicket and left the dun. He forded the stream and crept within a hundred yards of the buildings. Two horses stood hip-shot, but darkness prevented him from identifying the animals as Langley's blue roan and gray pack-horse. The door of the sod house hung wide open, and Bannister moved close so that he could see inside. When he reached the side of the barn, he saw two men seated at the table in the center of the house and recognized them as Crescent hands—the swarthy Sanchez and the blondish Buck.

He waited for some little while, making sure that he had only two men to deal with. Finally, convinced, he drew his revolver and moved quietly toward the house.

Buck was shuffling a greasy deck of cards when Bannister appeared in the doorway. He sat staring with his mouth agape. Sanchez twisted on the bench, looked over his shoulder and gasped, "*Por Dios*!"

Bannister said, "Sit still." He thumbed back the

Colt's hammer. "And, by damn, I mean still!"

Sanchez lay his hands palm down on the table and Buck still held the cards in that frozen attitude. It seemed to Bannister that fear was an odor in the room. He stepped inside, lifted Sanchez's gun from its holster and flung it outside. He went around the table and followed suit with Buck's weapon. Their saddle-guns leaned against the wall to one side of the door, and he disposed of them in the same way. He went to the end of the table.

"What happened to my partner, Buck?"

The Crescent man looked surprised. "I don't know, Bannister," he said thickly, and his gaze returned to Bannister's cocked gun. "And that's the honest truth."

"You haven't seen him?"

"Not since that day we jumped him here."

"How long have you two been squatting here?"

"Since just before sundown," Buck said. "Harbeson sent us out here on the chance that you'd show up. We didn't figure you'd come, though. That's why you caught us off guard." He got over the worst of his fright, and said, with more boldness, "You must be loco, Bannister. If you had any sense, you'd be back in Texas by now instead of hanging around here after pulling such a lowdown stunt."

Bannister said, "What are you talking about, Buck?"

"About your back-shooting John Forbes," Buck said. "As if you didn't know!"

Bannister gave a start. "You telling it straight, Buck? Somebody shot John Forbes?"

It was Sanchez who answered, his voice ugly with hatred. "Quit playing dumb, Bannister. We know you killed the dude, and you can't tell us different."

Bannister eyed him narrowly, remembering that it had been Sanchez who used the whip on Will Langley and Sanchez who refused to untie him when Buck suggested it that day they turned him loose in the sand flats. He said, "You say another word, Sanchez, and I'll drive your teeth down your throat with the barrel of this gun." He eased the hammer off cocked position and readied the gun. Then he looked at Buck. "Let's hear the rest of it."

Buck said, "You fooling, Bannister?"

Bannister said, "I'm not fooling around with you any longer, friend. Talk up. Don't make me beat it out of you."

Buck threw down the deck of cards and several of them struck the lantern on the center of the table, the room's only illumination. He said, "A man named Parsons from Dalton came upon the Crescent buckboard a couple miles from town. The grays were stopped, but they'd been running hard—blowing and lathered. Parsons looked around for a driver. He didn't see anybody. He decided to backtrack the team. He found Forbes out by the Graveyard, where he was bush-whacked—dead. Back-shot. Am I telling you something you don't know, Bannister?"

"You are."

Buck said, "I'll bet," and Sanchez sneered.

Bannister was silent now, shocked. At the moment he failed to catch the significance of this pair's assumption that he had killed Forbes. He thought of the Crescent manager, the only man in these parts who wasn't a man of violence, dead by a shot fired into his back. He thought of Helen Forbes, and wondered how she was taking it. Hard, he was sure. She at least was a woman of deep feelings. She would be suffering. Bannister still held his gun steady, but Sanchez saw that he wasn't on guard now. With a quick slash of his arm, Sanchez knocked the lantern off the table. Its glass shattered on the floor and its flame was extinguished. Bannister lashed out with his gun, but in the darkness he missed the man. Sanchez leapt for the doorway and plunged outside.

Bannister went after him, clubbing with his revolver as Sanchez grabbed for a gun on the ground. He missed the blow, but collided with the Crescent man and bowled him over. Sanchez landed on his side, heaved over in a roll, came cat-quick to his feet. He fired as Bannister rushed him again.

CHAPTER TWELVE

Bannister was a moving target and Sanchez fired with too much haste, so, despite the almost pointblank range, the shot missed. And before the Crescent man could fire again, the barrel of Bannister's Colt clouted Sanchez hard to the left temple and stretched him out loosely on the ground. Bannister whipped around toward the doorway, expecting the other Crescent hand to come rushing out at him. Buck came slowly, his hands held shoulder high.

"You kill him, Bannister?"

"No. He fired the shot." Bannister swore. "I should have killed the bastard. He's had it coming to him for a long time." The thought passed through his mind that he was letting too many of his enemies live to make trouble for him, but he still couldn't bring himself to kill in cold blood. He said, "He's harmless for a little while, but you're not. Walk ahead of me. I don't want you grabbing up a gun and trying to back-shoot me."

Buck obeyed, walking across the yard.

Bannister took him along to the creek, and across it. There he mounted his horse, holstered his gun, and said, "Not that you'll believe it, but you'd better look elsewhere for Forbes's bushwhacker. I didn't kill him."

"I'm beginning to think you didn't, Bannister."

"Who claimed I did—Matt Harbeson?"

"Yeah. He said you'd threatened Forbes."

"Well, I did threaten him, when I first came here. But that was before I found out Harbeson bossed Crescent," Bannister said. "A threat is no evidence of murder, Buck. Harbeson just saw a chance to make more trouble for me." A sudden thought came, and wouldn't be ignored. "Where was Harbeson at the time Forbes was killed?"

"Out on the range with the rest of us," Buck said. "If you're thinking Matt killed the dude, you're on the wrong track. What reason would he have?"

Bannister shrugged. "I don't know," he said, and turned away.

He rode east through the darkness, bound for Dalton. The news of the murder would have reached the town by now, and he felt he must tell Janet and Ben Maury that he hadn't done it. And he had to get word to Helen Forbes—through the Maurys, maybe—that he hadn't killed her husband. Somehow that seemed even more important than convincing Janet and Ben of his innocence.

Despite the late hour, Dalton was still wide awake when he arrived. Every house and building appeared to be lighted, and he saw, without entering it, that the single street was lined with saddle horses and rigs and that men stood talking in small groups. He knew that the word had spread far across the Strip, and, since the murder of such a man as John Forbes was big news, morbid curiosity had brought many riders into town. Taking care not to be seen, he went as usual to the rear of the Maury building. Ben opened the door to his knock.

"Jim, you shouldn't have come here!"

Bannister stepped inside and closed the door. "Where's Janet?"

"She went to Crescent. She thought Helen Forbes would need her."

"I just heard about her husband and—"

"Lord, Jim, why'd you do it?"

"I didn't."

"But everybody says—"

"I didn't kill John Forbes," Bannister said. "I came here to tell you and Janet. Harbeson jumped at the chance to pin it on me, Ben. Sure, I once made a threat against Forbes—but not to shoot him in the back. And it wasn't a threat I intended to carry out, after I learned that he didn't run Crescent Ranch."

"But who did kill him, if you didn't?"

"How should I know?" Bannister said savagely. He knew that he hadn't convinced Maury of his innocence. "How could anybody know, in a country like this? I had a hunch Harbeson did it, but a Crescent hand told me he was out on the range with his crew, and the man seemed to be

152

telling the truth. Maybe somebody killed him to rob him. Was Forbes's money gone?"

"No."

"Ben, you still think I did it, don't you?"

"Jim, I don't like to think you're a liar, but you're as reckless a man as I've ever known. You've had a raw deal from Crescent and—" He broke off, seeing the rock-hard look on Bannister's face. "You're right," he said, in an altered tone. "I shouldn't find you guilty on such flimsy evidence. And as far as I'm concerned, your word is better than Matt Harbeson's. But it's not me you've got to worry about. The whole countryside is aroused. Harbeson has posted a reward of a thousand dollars for you, dead or alive, and nine of ten men in No Man's Land will be gunning for you."

"So that's why this town is swarming with men?"

"That's it. Harbeson has set up headquarters in O'Leary's Saloon and he's organizing a systematic manhunt. He's not letting the riders chase all over the Strip. He's sending them out in small groups to fine-comb the country. He even plans to supply them with grub so they can stay out until you're caught. He told me to keep the store open, so I could sell them what they need."

Bannister said bitterly, "Well, you'll get some benefit out of this mess, anyway."

"I'd rather not profit in this fashion," Maury

said. "Jim, I know you're not a man to take advice, but I'm going to give you some anyway. Ride out before the manhunt starts. Strike out for Texas, and don't stop until you're a hundred miles below the line."

Bannister said, "I guess I've got no choice," and turned to the door.

He mounted his horse, then looked back at Maury.

"Tell Janet that I didn't kill Forbes," he said. "Ask her to tell Mrs. Forbes that."

Maury nodded, but Bannister had no faith in the gesture.

Away from town, he rode in the direction of Crescent Ranch. The only way he could convince Janet and Helen Forbes of his innocence was to see them himself.

At Crescent headquarters, despite the lateness of the hour when he arrived, Bannister found the bunkhouse lighted and a lantern burning inside the doorway of the barn. This meant that not all the hands were out manhunting him. At the main house, the window blinds were drawn, as a symbol of mourning, but lamps glowed behind them. Reining in at the edge of the yard, Bannister wondered if he had done right in coming here at such a time.

After debating with himself for a few minutes, he circled to the rear of the house and dismounted.

He went to the kitchen door and knocked lightly, and immediately Janet's voice said, "Who is it?"

"Jim, Janet."

He thought he heard her gasp. She opened the door and said, "Jim, you shouldn't have come here!" Her voice was off key with alarm.

He closed the door and removed his hat, looking at her in a searching way. She was wearing an apron. On the table stood a teapot, and a cup and saucer on a tray. He supposed she was preparing the tea for Helen Forbes. Her expression told him nothing except that his presence here upset her.

"Jan, you don't believe such a thing of me, do you?"

"I don't want to, Jim."

"It's not true. I didn't kill John Forbes."

She locked her fingers together and twisted them. "Everyone says it was you, and I—I guess I let them convince me. You see, Jim, all I really know about you is that—well, that you've brought nothing but trouble to this part of the Strip." She shook her head, and tears welled in her eyes. "But I don't want to believe such a thing of you, darling."

He said, "I don't blame you for believing it when everyone told you I killed him, but I thought you'd take my word against the whole world's."

"You once threatened him, Jim."

"Yes, I'm guilty of that."

"I begged you not to go on fighting Crescent."

"You did," he said. "And maybe I should have done as you asked. Still, I had to play the game in my own way."

She turned from him, got the tea kettle from the stove and moved to the table to pour water into the teapot. Not looking at him, Janet said, "You made a mistake in not finding a new range when Matt Harbeson first told you not to settle at Boot Creek. But you wanted to defy him more than you wanted to secure your future. Now you've lost everything—your range, your cattle, and your life if you don't leave No Man's Land and at once." She did look at him then, and she shuddered. "Jim, I think I'll lose my reason if I have to go on worrying. Are you going to let them catch you—hang you?"

His face had turned rocky. "Until right now I didn't know what I'd do," he said. "Now I know. Somebody's got to find out who killed Forbes. And since nobody else is bothering, it's got to be me."

"That means you won't leave No Man's Land?"

"Not with this hanging over me."

"Jim, you have no hope, at all. You'll be caught—"

"I won't be caught," he said. "I've got a hideout in the hills south of Boot Creek range, and I can always hole up there if I'm in danger. And in the meantime, I'll find a way to get at the one man who may know something about Forbes's murder—Matt Harbeson."

"You think he—"

"I don't think he fired the shot. But he could have hired somebody to do it."

"But why, Jim? Why?"

"I don't know, but I intend to find out," he said. "How is Mrs. Forbes taking it?"

"She's like a person in a daze," Janet said. "She sits in her room and stares at nothing. She doesn't cry. She won't eat or sleep. I'm taking a cup of tea to her now, hoping she'll drink it. The funeral will be an ordeal for her, I know."

"I wish there was something I could do."

"There's nothing anybody can do, Jim."

"When it's easier for her, later on," he said, "you'll tell her I'm not the one who killed him?"

"Yes. And now you'd better go."

"All right, Janet."

"You won't do as I ask—save yourself?"

"I'll do my best to save myself," he said. "But not in the way you ask."

He waited, but Janet didn't reply. She just stood there with her head bowed. He turned and went out, sick at heart. There was no longer anything between him and Janet.

Nothing at all.

He mounted and rode away from Crescent. The night was quiet. But by morning, No Man's Land would be swarming with manhunters bent on taking him, dead or alive.

CHAPTER THIRTEEN

Each morning, Matt Harbeson told himself, "Today ought to do it." Each night, he was disappointed. No rider came racing into Crescent headquarters with the news that Bannister had been found. Ten days had passed since the funeral, yet nobody had even cut sign of the hunted man—this in spite of the thousand dollar bounty on him, and despite the fact that Harbeson had sent men down into Texas, to make sure Bannister hadn't left the Strip.

Still, with so many men gunning for him, Bannister couldn't escape. And meanwhile, everything else was working out to Harbeson's satisfaction.

He was seated more firmly in the saddle at Crescent Ranch than ever before. The arrival of J. P. Vorhees hadn't altered that. He'd had one talk with the company bigwig, and the old man had placed all the blame on Bannister. Now Vorhees had sent for him again, and Harbeson crossed the ranchyard toward the house with an almost jaunty stride.

His conscience bothered him not at all. Actually, the longer the manhunt continued and the more he talked of Bannister as the murderer, the less real the truth seemed and he found it increasingly easy to blot from his mind the fact that he'd fired the fatal shot.

True, he had yet to face Helen Forbes. He hadn't seen her since the day of the funeral at Dalton. She'd returned to Crescent with the Maury girl, and shut herself up in her room. He had it from Janet Maury that Helen would stay with her in town later on, until she was able to plan her future, and that was something he didn't like. He'd taken it for granted that Helen would stay on at Crescent, and that her future would be entwined with his own. He would have to talk with her, when the time was right.

Entering the house, he hoped for a meeting with Helen. But he could hear her and Janet Maury talking upstairs. He turned to the study where old Vorhees sat at the desk where John Forbes had spent so much of his time, hesitating on the threshold until the man said, crankily, "Come in, Harbeson. Don't stand there like a bashful schoolboy."

Harbeson stepped into the room, removing his hat. It annoyed him to admit, even to himself, that this old man made him feel uneasy. Vorhees was frail, pale, wrinkled, and snow-white of hair and sideburns. In his rusty black suit, he might have been mistaken for a retired clerk and no more formidable than an ancient church deacon. But he was worth many millions, and Matt Harbeson, for all his toughness, was awed by wealth.

Vorhees said, "There's no news?"

"No, sir."

"I don't like it, Harbeson. I don't like it, at all."

"We'll get him soon, sir. I'd gamble on it."

"I'm not a gambling man, myself," Vorhees said. "I'm not becoming one at this late date. I've decided to take two steps that should assure the capture of this murderer. First, I'm increasing the reward offer to five thousand dollars."

"Good. That'll speed things up for sure."

"Second, I'm going to employ the Pinkerton Agency."

"There's no need for that, Mr. Vorhees." Harbeson's uneasiness increased, and began to show. "Once I spread word that the bounty on Bannister's hide is five thousand dollars, they'll tear No Man's Land apart."

"I don't share your belief that Bannister is still in No Man's Land," Vorhees said dryly. "In fact, I have no confidence that you appreciate the kind of man you're up against. He's devilishly clever, Harbeson. Too clever for you and all the men you've got looking for him. That's why I intend to bring in Pinkerton detectives. I'll write a letter to the Agency's office at Chicago immediately. Have a rider ready to take it to Dalton, so that it goes out on the next stage."

Harbeson nodded. "Whatever you say."

"Meanwhile, get out word of the five-thousand-dollars reward," Vorhees said. "And tell your manhunters to look farther afield than No Man's Land. I'm convinced that Bannister has fled this part of the country, but I want him apprehended no matter if he's gone to Timbuktu. That will be all for now, Harbeson."

Harbeson said, "Yes, sir," and left the study.

Crossing the hall, he heard light footsteps on the stairs. It wasn't Helen Forbes, however, but Janet Maury. Feeling cheated, he went out. On the porch he stopped to roll and light a cigarette and to think over his talk with the old man. The increased reward offer suited him fine. It should get results. But he didn't like the idea of bringing in Pinkerton detectives.

No regular officers ventured into the Neutral Strip, but occasionally the Pinkertons made a foray into the country, and they never left it empty-handed. Harbeson had encountered some of the Agency's operatives, Charlie Siringo for one, and they didn't fool easily. He didn't want them prowling around. They might learn too much for his comfort.

He saw the kid Sherry shoeing a horse at the blacksmith shed. Sherry had recovered from the wound Bannister had given him, but he still nursed his grudge against the Texan. Harbeson crossed to the shed.

He said, "Kid, saddle a bronc for a trip to Dalton. The old man wants a letter put on the next stage out of the Strip." He gave Sherry a

161

five-dollar gold piece. "Have a few drinks on me, eh?"

Sherry eyed him with surprise. Harbeson grinned.

"If you should happen to lose that letter on the way," he said, "don't bother to mention it when you get back."

For Jim Bannister it was a nightmarish game of hide and seek, and he needed as much luck as skill to keep from being tagged out. After his talk with Janet at Crescent Ranch, he had most of that night left before the game started in earnest. He'd returned to the hideout camp in the hills and cooked enough food to last several days, on short rations. Then he'd moved the remainder of his provisions and his camp gear away from the spring. The new cache was in a brush-grown ravine, where it was less likely to be discovered. He'd also hidden his saddle there, and driven his horse out onto the range. He liked the idea of being afoot no more than any man born to the saddle, but he'd decided to locate a hiding place where horses could not travel and the manhunters wouldn't expect a riding man to go. That had seemed to be his only chance of eluding them.

He'd found such a place, a rocky shelf eighty feet up a sheer cliff about half a mile from his former camp. There he lay hidden each day, while riders swarmed through the hills.

The first three days had been the worst, because

then the manhunters were most numerous and eager. At times some passed along the base of the slope, so close that their voices floated up to him, and he would lie among the rocks, clutching his rifle and sweating. Then, with hills fine-combed, most of them searched elsewhere. But no day passed without Bannister seeing or hearing at least one group or pair of hunters, and each night when he crept from hiding, he saw the glare of campfires in the hills.

He came out at night to stretch his cramped muscles, and to go to the spring to drink. Two nights he found men camped at the spring, and had to go without water. He rationed himself as to food, a couple of stale biscuits and a piece of bacon twice a day. He grew gaunt. Even after eating he felt half starved. But he stuck it out, and though he couldn't be sure of the exact number of days, he supposed that it had been two weeks.

And he was still safe.

Twice he had gone to the ravine to cook more of his dwindling supply of food, kindling his fire among some rocks and killing it as soon as the grub was ready. Finally he made another trip to the ravine only to find that some varmints had raided his cache. They had eaten all of the bacon and when he picked up the gnawed flour sack, what little flour remained spilled onto the ground. Abruptly he felt hungrier than at any time during the two weeks, because of the knowledge that he was without food, and all he could think of now was the need to get something to eat no matter what risk he ran.

He'd left a large stock of provisions at his ranch headquarters, but the chances of finding food in the house at this late date seemed very remote. With so many men prowling the country, somebody must have raided his cupboard. Or Crescent hands could have destroyed or removed the grub so he would go hungry. Still, with his mind's eye, he could see the canned goods, coffee, slabs of bacon, sacks of flour . . . He grabbed up his rifle and saddlebags, and set out for Boot Creek.

He saw no campfires in the hills tonight, but an hour later, coming onto the range, he saw the glimmer of one to the west. It bothered him hardly at all, with his mind so preoccupied with thoughts of food, and now, trusting to the darkness for protection, he set out at a dogtrot.

That pace couldn't be maintained for long, however; not by a horseman unaccustomed to traveling afoot. Seldom-used muscles soon tired, high-heeled boots made the going more difficult, and weakness brought on by hunger soon had him winded. Even after he slowed to a walk, he had to rest frequently.

Once, while he rested, he heard a rider somewhere behind him, but the beat of hoofs soon faded in the distance. It was long past midnight when he reached Boot Creek, almost completely spent. He drank, and rested. Then, fording the stream, he approached his buildings at a stumbling walk. He recalled that Sanchez and Buck had been posted here on his last visit, but tonight the corral held no horses and as he reached the side of the sod house, he sensed that it too was empty.

He entered, closed and barred the door. He placed rifle and saddlebags on the table, then in the darkness felt his way to the cupboard near the stove. The shelves were still laden with provisions.

Bannister threw caution aside. He found the lantern that Sanchez had knocked to the floor. The glass shade was broken, but the base still contained oil and the wick took a flame. He set the lantern on the table, hardly giving it a thought that his light, dim though it was, could be seen through the windows by any riders who might come within a mile of the place. In a frenzy of haste, he kindled a fire and set about preparing a solid meal.

By the time he'd eaten and cooked up a second batch of grub to carry in his saddlebags, dawn was too near for him to return to the hills. Crossing open range after daylight, he would be easy game for the manhunters whose campfire he'd seen on his way here. It occurred to him that his ranch headquarters might be as safe a hiding place as any, at least for a little while. Riders must have come here so often looking for him that they no longer gave it a thought. At any rate, he preferred staying there to being in the open at daybreak.

He'd had to fetch water from the creek to make coffee, and there was still a lot left in the pail. He got a bar of yellow soap from the cupboard, then stripped down and gave himself a badly needed scrubbing. He got his razor from the saddlebags, lathered his face and scraped off his wiry growth of bristle. He had no clean clothing, since his gear was hidden in the ravine, but even so he felt less like a hunted animal for having eaten well and slicked up a bit.

He blew out the lamp flame finally, and then it was gray dawn outside. He stretched out on his bunk, not falling asleep at once but thinking, for the first time in two weeks, of what lay ahead.

He had to admit that his hiding out had gained him nothing. The manhunt had been far more determined and long-lasting than he'd anticipated. It had forced him to crawl into a hole, and even now he dared not come out into the open. The search was still on. He would have done better by fleeing No Man's Land.

But even as that thought occurred to him, he rejected it. He wouldn't run. Like so many other poor fools, he was willing to fight and even die for his stake in life. There was nothing heroic about it. Countless men had done it on the frontier and in the cattle country, for smaller stakes than his. And he couldn't have any peace of mind with this rigged murder charge hanging over him. And it would always be there, no matter how far he ran. Unless he did something about it.

What could he do, though?

It had seemed simple enough, the night he'd talked with Janet at Crescent Ranch. He'd believed that Matt Harbeson had a hand in it, and that he only needed to get at the man to force an admission from him. That had been a fool's daydream. In reality, a hunted man did no hunting, and Harbeson was safe from him. He wasn't sure now that Harbeson had been the murderer. Maybe Harbeson had just seen his chance to make things tough for Jim Bannister, after somebody else with a grudge against Crescent back-shot John Forbes.

Bannister lay there wondering what his next move should be, and a part of his mind kept insisting that he mustn't discard his plan to tackle Matt Harbeson. A sixth sense seemed to be telling him that Harbeson was the key to his problem, the way out for him. And he found himself asking, why can't the hunted become the hunter?

As he grew drowsy, he made his decision: he would go after Matt Harbeson.

He slept until midafternoon, and awoke to

hunger again. He began to think that his appetite would never be satisfied. More cautious now, he didn't kindle a fire because smoke rising from the chimney could be seen for miles. He ate cold leftover beans and drank what coffee remained in the pot. He built a smoke, then ventured outside. Scanning the range in every direction, he saw no riders. He looked for his remuda, and for a time thought that the Maugher crowd must have taken his horses when they stole his herd. But finally he caught sight of the animals far to the southwest. He wanted a mount badly, but knew that he should wait until after sundown to try to catch one.

Today the waiting went hard. He felt restless, now that he was well-fed and had been on the move again, and he knew that he wouldn't be able to stand the strain of going back into hiding. When the sun finally set, he started out with his rifle, saddlebags and a rope. He aimed directly toward the half-dozen horses, which now were grazing about a mile to the south. They became aware of him long before he came within roping distance, and he began to fear that they would bolt when he drew closer. His dun, the best horse in his brand, wasn't among them, but he saw the little gray gelding that he'd used as a pack-horse when he took Will Langley into the hills.

He thought of Langley as he lay down his rifle and saddlebags. Will must have gone back to

Texas, after all. He reflected wryly that Langley had shown good sense. A hundred yards away from the horses now, he shook out his loop. They were fat and sleek from not being worked, but spooky too. They had stopped grazing. They watched him with their ears flicked forward, and one, a big bay, snorted and stamped as though threatening to fight.

Bannister decided on the bay, and moved forward a few steps. He halted, called softly, "Hello, boy. Stand still, you handsome devil." The bay gelding pawed the ground, tossing its head. It acted like a stallion, and Bannister chuckled. "Steady, you faker. Steady, boy!"

He kept moving in, a few steps at a time, and at last was close enough. He readied his loop, then broke into a run. The bay trumpeted and the entire bunch wheeled away. Bannister made his throw, bracing himself as the loop encircled the bay's heavy-maned neck. The rope snapped taut, but with such force that it jerked him off his feet. He clung to the lariat, but the bay began running and started to drag him. He scrambled up, but toppled again. He had no choice but to let go of the rope. He rose slowly this time, and then beyond the fleeing horses he saw a rider.

Fear had him by the throat. For a moment he was too shaken to grab for his gun.

CHAPTER FOURTEEN

By the time Bannister got his gun out, he realized that there were no other riders, and this one was not threatening him. The man swung after the remuda, singling out the bay, his rope ready. He made his throw, catching the bay and bringing it to a rearing halt.

It was Jubal Kane.

The old man came along with the bay in tow, and the horse, already over the notion that it had become a wild stallion, was docile enough and didn't fight the rope. Kane reined in, smiled, and said, "Looks like I showed up in time, this time, bucko."

"Yeah. You're Johnny-on-the-Spot."

"Always glad to lend a hand."

Bannister went to the bay and removed Kane's rope from its neck, then fashioned his own rope into a *bosal* so he could ride the horse. He swung onto the animal, which instantly bucked him off its bare back. He kept his hold on the free end of the *bosal* and gave the horse several smart blows with the flat of his hand. It bucked with less enthusiasm after that. He rode to his rifle and saddlebags, dismounted to pick them up, and by the time he mounted again, Kane had rejoined him.

Bannister said, "Don't tell me somebody sent you to help me again. This time I won't be able to believe it."

"Somebody did."

"Who, old man? Not the same person?"

"Who else?"

"You're forgetting there's a thousand-dollar bounty on my hide?"

"A five-thousand-dollar bounty, bucko."

"Oh? So they've raised the ante?"

"That's right," Kane said. "One of the company bigwigs came out from Philadelphia and he figures it's worth that much to nail your hide to the fence."

"You had your chance a couple minutes ago. Why'd you pass it up?"

Jubal Kane shrugged. "What's money to me? I'm sixty-seven years old. A good man for that age, but no horny young buck. What could I buy with all that money that would do me any good? All I want is a good job and the health to work at it. Trouble is, I'm not going to have a job much longer if I have to keep on playing nursemaid to you. But you're a hard man to find, Bannister. I've been prowling those hills for three days, and wouldn't have found you now except by luck. I was on my way home when I saw you. I'd begun to figure you weren't in the hills, like I'd been told."

"Who told you I was holed up there?"

"Mrs. Forbes."

"How'd she know?"

"You told the Maury girl, and she told the widow."

"How is she, Jubal?"

"Who? The widow or the Maury girl?"

"Mrs. Forbes. She's the one who's had the rough time."

"All right I reckon," Kane said. "She bears up. She's got a lot of spunk. She wants to see you."

"What about?"

"She didn't say. You coming?"

"Sure. Where and when do we meet her?"

"At an abandoned homesteader place a couple miles southeast of Dalton." Kane told Bannister how to find the place. "It'll be sometime tonight, I guess, after I've let her know I've found you. She's staying with the Maurys nowadays. I'll head for town now. You'll be there?"

Bannister nodded. He would indeed be there.

After Kane left, Bannister picked up his saddle at the ravine in the hills, and then, properly mounted, set out for the rendezvous. He felt eager for the meeting. In fact, the prospect of seeing Helen Forbes filled him with excitement. This seemed strange, considering how fond of Janet Maury he had been until he realized that she would never understand him—nor approve of him, either, for that matter. Or perhaps it wasn't strange, at all. He had looked upon Helen

Forbes and found her to his liking, so much so that he had imagined that one day, when he became a successful cattleman, he would have a woman like her for his wife. Then, after at least half convincing himself that such a woman was not for him, he had turned to Janet, who on the surface seemed more his kind. Actually, he'd fallen under Helen's spell, and now he was in its grip again. Just as Janet wouldn't do for him, no woman *like* Helen would do. He knew the truth at last. He wanted Helen, not a substitute. Only she could make him complete, as a man needed to be.

Such thinking could only lead to a dead end, however. She was a widow now, but that didn't bring her within his reach. Her bid to talk with him didn't mean that she hated him any less. In her eyes, he would still be Jim Bannister, a Texas gunman. She might even want to accuse him to his face of murdering her husband. What else would she have to say to him?

He had far to go so he traveled at a steady lope, the big bay covering mile after mile without a break in its stride. Beyond the sand flats, he crested a rise and almost rode down into a camp beyond it. He saw the red-glowing embers of a dying fire just in time to swerve away from the spot. One of the men leaped from his blankets, gun in hand, and shouted, "Who's there?"

Bannister didn't answer quickly enough, for

when he called out, "Crescent!" the man yelled, "Like hell!" and drove a shot at him. He touched spurs to the bay, and it stretched out in a gallop. Glancing back, he saw three shadowy figures running for their horses. But the men there had to saddle up, and they never found him in the darkness.

He covered perhaps fifteen miles in about two hours, and arrived at the homesteader place with the bay lathered and blowing. It was in a broad hollow, the usual house and barn of sod. The roof of the house had caved in, and one wall of the barn was crumbling away. Grass was beginning to grow again in the plowed fields and the whole place made a sorry monument to somebody's faded dreams. He found the only water available in a stone-walled well in the middle of the yard. After the bay finished blowing, Bannister drew a pail of water and let the horse drink.

He waited in the deep shadows at the side of the barn, hunkered down with his back to the wall, and smoked a cigarette. He kept thinking of Helen Forbes, wondering what she wanted of him and puzzling over his eagerness to see her. It was odd, how his mind could conjure up the picture of her with such startling clarity. She seemed far more real to him than Janet Maury, whom he knew so much better. He couldn't get around the fact that she wasn't for him, but another fact had to be faced: she would live in his memory the rest of his days, be they many or few.

Around midnight, he heard the clatter of hoofs and creak of wheels. Then he saw a topless buggy loom through the darkness. Janet was with Helen, handling the reins. She stopped the horse a little distance from the house and called, "Jim, are you there?"

He rose and stepped away from the barn. "I'm here, Janet."

He walked toward the rig, approaching the side where Helen Forbes sat. He removed his hat and said, "Good evening, Mrs. Forbes. Janet, how are you?"

Janet alone replied, saying, "Quite well, Jim. And you?"

He said, "I make out," and then he met Helen's eyes. His heart heat faster, and he could feel the swift coursing of blood in his veins. He said, "Mrs. Forbes, the news of your husband's death was a shock to me. I don't know the right word, so I can only say that I am sorry."

She said tonelessly, "Will you help me down, please?"

He gave her a hand, and after she alighted she turned away and walked past the sod house to the well. He followed, and when she faced him he saw how pale she was. She looked as though she had forgotten how to smile. But she was still beautiful in Bannister's eyes, and infinitely desirable. She was slow to speak, and he didn't know what to say to this woman who, through no design of her own and entirely against his will, had become so important in his life.

Finally she said, "Janet told me that you deny murdering my husband. I want you to deny it to me."

"I deny it, but I don't think it's necessary. You must know I wouldn't be able to face you if I'd killed him."

"I don't know that at all."

"How can I convince you?"

She didn't answer, but studied him intently for several minutes. He submitted to her scrutiny with a surface calm that belied the excitement he felt.

At last she said, "I suppose I am convinced, Bannister. No doubt I was convinced all along, and I came to meet you because I needed to tell you so. It's been hard for you?"

"Not as hard as it's been for you."

"You've thought of me?"

"Yes. A great deal."

She looked at him in that searching way again. "I don't know what to make of you," she said. "My mind tells me you're vicious, a brute. Yet I feel that you're something else. That you have decent instincts."

He had no comment for that. Taking out tobacco sack and papers, he began shaping up a smoke, eyeing her wonderingly while about it. She wore

176

a light coat against the night chill, its wide collar turned up at the back of her neck. It had two big patch pockets, and her right hand was thrust into one. She'd kept it there all the while they'd been together, he'd noticed. He lighted his cigarette, studying her in the glare of the match. Her face had grown thin since their last encounter, making her eyes seem enormous.

He said, "Did you have another reason for wanting to see me?"

"You're very sharp, Bannister."

"I have a feeling that you want something of me."

"Now that I'm convinced that you're not the murderer, I do want something. Do you have any idea who the murderer is?"

"I have a suspicion."

"Matt Harbeson, Bannister?"

He gave a start, and stared at her with surprise. "Yes, Matt Harbeson," he said. "That was a good guess. Or was it more than a guess? Do you suspect him?"

"I find myself thinking that if you're not the guilty man, he must be."

"Why?" he asked. "Why do you think he must be?"

"He had as much motive as you. Perhaps even more."

"Such as?"

"My husband sent a telegram to J. P. Vorhees,

one of the officers of the Crescent Cattle Company, informing him of the situation here," she said. "At the time of John's death, Mr. Vorhees was on his way here—and Harbeson knew it. He also knew Mr. Vorhees wouldn't approve of his acts of violence—against you and against others before you. He knew John would tell the whole story, and Mr. Vorhees would certainly investigate. I think it possible that Harbeson feared he would lose his job, or at least that he would no longer have a free hand at Crescent. If I'm right, he murdered my husband to silence him. And by blaming you, he made it appear that you were the troublemaker and he was justified in taking steps against you. At the same time, he must have seen that a manhunt would dispose of you. Or at least he hoped it would. And if that isn't enough motive, there's also the fact that—" She fell silent, biting down on her lower lip. "Well, never mind that."

Bannister dragged hard on his cigarette. He said, "You and I are the only ones who suspect him, and we can't prove a thing."

"I want him found out and punished."

"And I'm going to help you with him?"

"It's to your advantage. By finding the murderer, you'll clear yourself."

He nodded. "That's true. But I have it from a Crescent hand named Buck that at the time of the murder Harbeson was on the range with the

Crescent crew. If he's guilty, he didn't fire the shot. He hired somebody to do the killing. Still, he's not above doing that. He hired some tough hands to make an attempt on my life the day I arrived at Boot Creek." He fell silent a moment, thinking. "If I'm to help you, you'll have to tell me everything—not hold back. What other reason did he have for wanting John Forbes dead?"

She avoided his gaze. "I'd rather forget that, Bannister."

"Maybe you can't afford to forget it. Look— have you reason to think that Harbeson wants you?"

She winced slightly. "You are sharp," she said, and added reluctantly, "It's just a feeling I have. Because of the way he looks at me. Because of the tone of his voice when he talks to me."

Bannister felt anger stir in him. "He's our man," he said, "but I don't know what can be done. I've had a notion that I could catch him alone somehow, and force him to admit his part in the murder. It's a fool notion at best. I'm likely to be the one who gets caught, with everybody manhunting me."

"I'll go back to Crescent Ranch tomorrow and talk with Mr. Vorhees. I'll tell him you're not the murderer."

"It will be Harbeson's word against yours."

"I think Mr. Vorhees will take mine against his," Helen said. "At least, he'll give me a hearing and I'll be able to sow a seed of doubt in his mind. He's a fair-minded person, and if he's got reason to doubt—well, I feel certain that I can work out something. Perhaps a meeting between you and him, and once he's talked with you he should feel as I do about it, regarding you, if not where Harbeson is concerned. If he withdraws the reward offer and the manhunt ends, will you meet with him, Bannister?"

"Can I trust him? Remember, I don't know the man."

"You can trust him."

"All right, then. I'll meet him."

She nodded. "And then you and I will try to find a way to prove we're right about Matt Harbeson. Or prove we're wrong about him, if that's the case. And now I'd better leave. I don't want to keep Janet waiting too long."

Bannister stepped aside so she could move away from the well, but as she passed him he dropped his cigarette and caught hold of her right arm. She swung around to face him, but did not struggle or cry out. He said, "Easy. I won't hurt you," and drew her hand from the coat pocket. Clutched in her hand was a twin-barreled derringer pistol. He forced her grip from the vicious little weapon.

He said, "So you planned to kill me. If you'd had a feeling that I was lying, you'd have tried to use this on me."

She wilted visibly and shuddered. "That was in my mind," she said huskily. "Maybe I would have gone through with it, maybe I wouldn't. I don't know." She covered her face with her hands, and sobbed, "That makes me as bad as the murderer, doesn't it? I think I must be losing my reason!"

Bannister said, "Steady, Helen. Get hold of yourself."

He threw the derringer into the well, then took her by the wrists and drew her hands from her face. He hadn't planned what happened next. He pulled her to him and, without conscious thought, kissed her upon the mouth.

CHAPTER FIFTEEN

For a moment it was nothing. He'd taken Helen by surprise, and her lips were not even submissive. They lay cool and somehow untouched during the first instant of contact. Then they responded, perhaps because his own were man-rough and so demanding. Not only did her lips mate with his, but the whole of Helen strained against him. But that too was fleeting, and even as he tightened his arms about her, she wrenched away. Free of him, she took two backward steps. More, she lifted her hand and drew the back of it across her lips as though wiping away something unclean.

And Janet's voice came, saying, "Helen, I think we'd better go."

Janet had driven the rig in past the house and seen it all, and Bannister, though still somewhat dazed, could detect the sharp edge of fury in her voice. He continued to watch Helen, contrite now and feeling that he'd played the fool.

He said, "I won't say I'm sorry, Helen. I'm no good at dodging the truth. And the truth is, I want you."

She said wretchedly, "Because I'm a widow, I'm fair game. Is that it, Bannister?"

"I've had you in my thoughts from the first time I saw you."

"You make me feel cheap, common."

"I'm sorry for that. It's wrong. It's been wrong from the start. But it's not something I could help. Telling myself that you're not for me did no good."

Across the yard, Janet said, still in that furious way, "Helen, please!"

Helen turned toward her, then faced Bannister again. "I'll forget this happened," she said. "I want you to forget. You'll still do as I ask, help find out if Harbeson is the murderer?"

He nodded, and then she walked away. He followed her after a moment, and helped her into the buggy. He could feel Janet's burning gaze upon him, and he thought bleakly: Quit it, Jan. There was little enough between you and me, and you spoiled that.

With Helen seated, he stepped back.

"I'll send Jubal to you after I've seen Mr. Vorhees," Helen said. "Does he know how to get in touch with you?"

"Tell him to come into the hills at a point directly south of my ranch buildings," he said. "I'll watch for him after dark each night."

Janet said, "There's more trouble in this. Jim, will you never use your good judgment? If Helen gets Mr. Vorhees to withdraw his reward offer, you'll be free to get out of this mess." Her voice almost cracked with annoyance. "You'll be able to gather your cattle and find a new range—and never again need to fight Crescent. But if you do as Helen wants, you'll go on fighting until either you or Matt Harbeson is dead. Don't you realize that?"

"Janet, I made my decision a long time ago," he said mildly. "I won't be driven away from Boot Creek."

"Your decision," Janet said, venom in her tone, "and your choice." She lifted the reins, preparatory to driving away. "That's quite obvious. For your sake, I hope it's the right choice—but I doubt that."

She rein-slapped the horse, and the buggy rolled past Bannister.

He looked after them until darkness swallowed the rig, smarting under the girl's words. Still, she had spoken the truth. He had made his choice, and a lot of good it would do him. He'd held Helen in his arms, and all he'd got out of that was the knowledge that she couldn't bear to have him touch her. He went to his horse, tightened its cinches and rose to the saddle.

It was nearly dawn when Bannister bedded down. He fell into sound sleep at once, something a hunted man couldn't afford to do. He awoke at daybreak, and as he sat up, stretching and yawning, a voice said, "Take it easy, Bannister. Don't make me shoot you." It came from behind him, and sounded vaguely familiar. Fear got an icy grip on him. His gun lay beside him, within easy reach. He fought against an impulse to grab it up and whip around to face the speaker. But as the last cobwebby strands of sleep cleared from his brain, he realized that such a move would be suicidal.

The unseen man said, "Let's have a talk, not a gunfight, bucko."

He recognized the voice. "Keough?"

"Yeah."

"All right."

"Talk?"

"Sure."

Pat Keough stayed behind Bannister. The hardcase apparently put little trust in Bannister's word. He said, "That bounty offer is for you dead or alive. I could have shot you while you slept, and collected. You thinking of that?"

Bannister nodded. "Quit being scared of me," he said. "I'm not going to pull anything. You want to talk, so we'll talk. Let me get up and I'll move away from my gun."

"Slow and easy, bucko."

Bannister rose slow and easy, moved six feet away from his blankets and the gun, and turned to face Keough. The man stood spread-legged, a cocked gun in his hand. He was smiling, but his blue eyes were wary.

He said, "You're a tricky cuss, and I'm afraid to take chances with you. By the way, I got my guns back off the roof of your barn." He chuckled. "You don't mind?"

"You come here to tell me that?"

"Naw."

"What, then?"

"I had one hell of a time finding you," Keough said. "I found out from your partner, Will Langley, that you had a hideout camp here in these hills. But it wasn't where he said. I was beginning to think I'd never find you, then you rode past where I was bedded down last night. I didn't know it was you, of course. But I did some snooping and here we are."

Bannister frowned, puzzled. "What's this about Langley? I had an idea he went back to Texas. I haven't seen anything of him in weeks."

"He's up at Rawson Wells, in a tight spot," Keough said. "He showed up there, looking for you. He didn't tell who he was or what he was doing. He just hung around, keeping his ears open. Then Matt Harbeson showed up with the news that you'd killed Forbes. He spread word around that he would pay a thousand dollars for you, dead or alive. And he recognized Langley."

"Go on, man."

"Harbeson jumped him, but Langley swore he didn't know your whereabouts and hadn't seen you for a week or more. Harbeson had to believe him. Anyway, a lot of the boys from the Wells started chasing around in the hope of collecting that bounty on your hide. Langley sat tight. By that time he figured you were hiding out in the Faro Hills where you'd set up that camp for him. But he knew he'd better not try to get to you. Some of the boys that weren't out bounty-hunting were watching him close, and they'd have trailed him if he rode out. He didn't want to lead them to you."

"But he told you where I might be hiding."

"Yeah."

"How come?"

Keough grinned. "It's a long story. Will's smart, but every man can be outsmarted. You see, he was broke and I staked him to a couple of dollars so he could eat. He didn't eat. He got in a poker game and lost the jack. I gave him another stake. He got in another game. This time he had some luck and ended up with a couple hundred dollars. He paid me back the four dollars he owed me, and I took him on a binge. We got real friendly."

"So he talked?"

"Not then. It was later. Like I said, this is a long story."

Bannister said, "I'm listening."

Keough went on, "He's living the life of Riley on the stake he won, but still he's worrying about you. One night a week ago he saddled his horse and rode out of town, just to see what happened. It happened. A half-dozen hombres set out after him. Will acted like he was just giving his horse

187

a run, and then he went back to town. But the boys are pretty sure he could lead them to you. Anyway, I got friendly with him. But I didn't learn anything from him until I found out it wasn't you that murdered John Forbes."

Bannister all but shouted, "What's that?"

"Yeah. I know you didn't bushwhack Forbes. That's why I came looking for you. After I found out about it, I told Will Langley. There wasn't anything he could do, with those bounty-hungry hombres keeping an eye on him. So he took a chance on me. He told me about the hideout camp here in the Faro Hills and I came to tell you there's a way out."

"Keep talking, Pat."

"Sure. It happened like this. I was with Jake Maugher and the others the night you stampeded the herd we'd stolen. Later on, when we were loafing around the Wells, I asked Jake how come he didn't make another try at your J-Bar-B cattle. He was likkering up at the time, else he wouldn't have talked. He said Matt Harbeson had told him the morning Forbes was killed to go after them again, because you wouldn't break up the rustling a second time. He told Jake you'd be taken care of."

Keough finally eased his gun off cocked position and holstered it. He took out makings and talked as he rolled a cigarette.

"This made Jake wonder. They were talking at

Crescent headquarters, see, before Forbes was bushwhacked. Jake had gone to tell Harbeson how you got your herd away from us." He nodded. "Yeah, Harbeson put Jake up to stealing your cattle. Well, after Harbeson said you'd be taken care of, he rode out. A little later John Forbes drove out. Jake got an idea. He's got a tricky mind, that Maugher. He followed Forbes's buckboard, and he was about half a mile behind it when the dude drove past those rocks called the Graveyard. He heard the shot and saw Forbes fall from the rig. He ducked so the bushwhacker wouldn't see him. But he wanted a look at that hombre, so he left his horse in a buffalo wallow and Injunned toward the Graveyard on foot. A couple minutes later he saw the bushwhacker come riding from the rocks and head south."

Bannister said, "Who was it, Pat?"

"Can't you guess? Matt Harbeson."

"A Crescent hand told me Harbeson was with his crew at that time."

"That cowhand was keeping an eye on him every minute?"

"I reckon not."

Keough grinned briefly. "Like I said, Jake Maugher was drunk when he told me about it. After he sobered up, he didn't remember he told me. But that's why Jake's not bothering to run off your cattle—or chasing around trying to collect that bounty on you. He knows something he can cash on. He figures on making Harbeson pay plenty to keep what he knows to himself."

Bannister bit his lip thoughtfully. This was what he'd needed to hear. His suspicions of Harbeson had been right. Buck had made a mistake in thinking that the Crescent boss was with the crew at the time of the murder. It was an easy mistake to make. Buck had seen Harbeson nearby during much of the day, and so he'd taken it for granted that he'd not been far off at any time. Still, Jake Maugher's testimony would be valueless unless somebody forced him to present it to the one man who would make proper use of it—J. P. Vorhees.

"So he'll blackmail Harbeson," Bannister said. "That could get him killed."

"Not Jake. He's tricky. He'll take precautions when he braces Harbeson."

"I can't see my being able to use him as a witness."

"Will Langley and I talked it over," Keough said. "We figured you'd want to get hold of Maugher."

Bannister eyed him curiously. "How come, Pat? You could play Jake's game, force him to cut you in on the blackmail game. You're passing that up like you passed up collecting that bounty on me. Since when does a hombre like you hate money?"

"Put it down that I'm not very bright," Keough said. "Fooling aside, I'm not anxious to collect that kind of money. You had a chance to kill Jake and me that day we jumped you at Boot Creek, but you let us go. I can't forget that. Besides, I like Will Langley—and he thinks a lot of you. Sure, I'm no saint. I rustle some cattle and steal a few horses now and then. But I draw the line at dirty deals, and I figure you've been handed one."

"How do I get hold of Jake Maugher, Pat?"

"That'll take some doing. You'll need help."

"Where will I get help?"

"Will and I figured we'd give you a hand," Keough said. "Let's have some breakfast and then talk it over, eh?"

Helen Forbes drove from Dalton in a rented buggy at nine o'clock the morning after her meeting with Jim Bannister. She was in a troubled frame of mind, for more reason than one. Janet was angry with her. In fact, Helen had sensed this morning—at breakfast and while she was preparing to leave the Maury house—that the girl hated her. Janet always seemed a placid sort of person, and Helen had been shocked upon discovering the violence of her feelings when she was upset. And Janet had been very much upset since last night.

She'd tried to tell the girl, as they drove away from the homesteader place, that Bannister's taking her into his arms meant nothing. Janet had said fiercely, "It's always been you with him, from the very beginning. I knew what was going on the day you came to Dalton to give him his guns. And you encouraged it!"

Helen had said, "No, no!"

Then Janet had said a terrible thing. "The truth is, I don't believe either of you is really broken up over your husband's death!"

Helen had been too shocked to voice a denial, and even now she wondered how Janet could have thought such a thing. Driving through the sparkling early morning sunlight, her mood was bleak despite the pleasant day. She knew what she must do. She must leave No Man's Land, go back East. She had no one back in Philadelphia, no family and no close friends, but still she must get away from this country which brought out the evil in people.

It was changing her. Or so she feared. She found it difficult to be tolerant. She couldn't forgive Janet, even though she knew the girl had spoken out of jealousy. And worse still, seed of doubt had been planted in her mind, and she wondered if, deep inside her, she were not guilty in the way Janet said.

There was reason for guilt, she told herself. For one insane instant she'd responded to Jim Bannister's advances. She felt her cheeks burn as she recalled how she'd let her lips seek his, and how her body had strained to him. Even now she imagined that she could feel the roughness of his kiss and the iron hardness of his body. It had been but a kiss and an embrace, yet she'd never been so completely possessed.

She'd never been a woman wholly beloved. She was twenty-eight, and John had been fifty-three. The difference in their ages hadn't made their marriage difficult, but that had been because she took pains to adapt herself to her husband's ways. She had been working in a millinery shop, a girl without a family, on her own and earning a meager livelihood, when she met John Forbes. He'd been a teller in a bank controlled by Mr. Vorhees, and a mistake in her employer's account had brought him to the shop. Her employer had been out. John had waited. They'd talked. He'd seemed different from the few men she knew, a gentleman, and she'd accepted his invitation to dinner.

He hadn't swept her off her feet, but he had courted her with a persistence that convinced her of his love and finally deceived her into thinking that she loved him. The marriage hadn't been a mistake. It hadn't been a failure. But something had been lacking. John's ardor had soon cooled, and he'd soon become content to let companionship substitute for passion. She had been as he wanted her to be, and thus a good wife. But there had been times when she craved the warmth of love, and its denial made her feel less than complete as a woman.

Jim Bannister?

He'd come into her life against her will, and even that first day, when he helped her overcome her timidity about handling a team of horses, he had somehow managed to insinuate himself into her consciousness as no man ever had. And even while hating him for being a troublemaker—and, yes, a gunman—she'd wondered what manner of man he was. She didn't know what had attracted her: he was rugged rather than handsome, and certainly he was no gentleman. She supposed that the strength she saw in him, the virility, had been a challenge to her.

However, her reaction to Jim Bannister didn't mean that she hadn't been fond of John Forbes. Yes, that was it. She and John had been fond of each other, but not in love, as she understood the word. And after seven years of marriage with a man like John, she was a little afraid of love as she had experienced it, for a fleeting second, with Jim Bannister last night.

She continued to think of Janet Maury, of Jim Bannister, of her deceased husband, and of herself in this confused way during the long drive to Crescent Ranch. Along the way, she was forced to pass the rocky stretch known as the Graveyard—the spot where John had died—and as she drove by she did what she hadn't permitted herself to do all this while. She cried. She wept agonizingly, and after she cried herself out she knew that Janet was wrong about her. She was lonely and lost without John; she was broken up by his death. He'd been her life for seven years, and never for one moment had she considered any other life. She didn't want Jim Bannister or any other man.

She was a mile from Crescent headquarters when they picked her up, three riders who appeared from the south and gradually overtook her horse and buggy. They were Crescent hands, and one was Matt Harbeson. He swung his horse alongside the rig and lifted his hand in a mocking salute.

"Welcome back to Crescent," he said. "This is where you belong, and it's good that you realize it."

Helen didn't reply. She didn't even look at him.

He and the others escorted her to the ranch headquarters, and there, when she halted the buggy before the main house, she had to submit to Harbeson's helping her down. He held onto her arm after she was on the ground.

"Like I said," he told her, "this is where you belong."

She pulled away. "I'm not here to stay. You may as well know that."

He gestured toward her luggage tied to the rear of the buggy. "That way it looks you are. Anyway, don't make up your mind to leave in a hurry. I'm telling you how it is. This is where you belong."

"My luggage merely means that I left the Maurys."

"So? Well, you have no place else to go."

She said, "I haven't?" and added, "I'm going to say something to Mr. Vorhees that concerns you. Maybe you'd better come inside and hear it."

"I'm right with you, sweetheart," Harbeson said, and climbed the porch steps with her.

Old Mr. Vorhees was in the study, seated at the desk writing a letter. He laid aside his pen, stood, and greeted her pleasantly while studying her with some concern. He inquired about her health, and seemed relieved when she said, "I'm quite well, Mr. Vorhees."

"I'm glad. I was worried about you for a time. Is there something I can do for you?"

"I have something to say. I hope you'll hear me out."

"Of course I will. Sit down. Matt, pull up a chair for the lady."

"Thank you, but I prefer to stand to say this."

Vorhees said, "Very well, my dear." His pale, wrinkled face was expressionless but curiosity showed in his still lively eyes. "I take it that you want Matt to hear what you have to say."

"It concerns him," she said, but at the same time she somehow gave the impression that she was completely unaware of Harbeson's presence. She wore her dark-green suit and the jaunty little hat. She twisted her gloves in her hands in a betrayal of her nervousness, but otherwise she managed to appear calm enough. She said, "To begin with, I talked with Jim Bannister last night."

After a moment of taut silence, Harbeson swore under his breath, and Vorhees said, "Please go on, Helen."

"I'm convinced that he did not murder my husband."

"He denied murdering him?"

"Yes. And I believe him. I asked him to meet me. I was sure that if I saw him I could tell whether or not he was guilty. I don't think he could have faced me if he'd murdered John." She saw that the old gentleman was impressed. "I think that if you would talk to him, you too would be convinced of his innocence."

"He would meet with me?"

"Yes, of course," Helen said. "I came to arrange a meeting, if you'll agree to it. But it would mean withdrawing the offer of a reward so that he's free to come out of hiding. I feel that we've found him guilty without a trial, and—well, he should at least have a hearing."

Vorhees turned to Harbeson who had rolled and lighted a cigarette and lounged in the doorway of the room, puffing on it.

"What do you think of this, Matt?"

"I hate to say what I think of it," Harbeson

said. "But I'd better say it. There's more to her meeting Bannister than she's told. How'd she get in touch with him, when a couple hundred men have been hunting him without any luck? She didn't just bump into him by chance. What I think is that—" he paused, giving Helen a wicked look—"she's been in cahoots with him all the while. Yeah. I should have figured that out long ago. I had reason to suspect such a thing."

Helen stared at him now, defiantly.

He went on, enjoying the situation. "The day after Bannister came here and threatened John Forbes, I rode out to Boot Creek with some of the crew. We found her out there, alone with Bannister. Real chummy, they were. It's not something I like to tell on a lady, but it looks like it should be told. What do I think? I think, Mr. Vorhees, that she fell for the no-good and the two of them planned to make a widow of her—so they could play together."

Vorhees appeared scandalized. "Helen, is there any truth to this?"

She regarded Harbeson with horror. He'd outwitted her. More, he'd struck at what was a woman's most vulnerable spot. He'd beaten her, after all. She said thickly, "The only truth to it is that I did visit Bannister at Boot Creek. The rest of it is—"

"You see?" Harbeson said. "She admits she was carrying on with Bannister. And it looks to me as though he killed Forbes, with or without her knowledge, so that they'd be free to go on carrying on."

The old man said, in an agony of embarrassment, "Helen, I don't know what to think. If you can explain this—"

She could not. The words wouldn't come. Her throat constricted as if the brutal hand of Matt Harbeson was strangling her. She whirled toward the door. Harbeson stepped aside for her, and she ran from the room and the house. She ran across the porch and down the steps and to the horse and buggy. The two men who had ridden in with Harbeson stood there by their horses.

Harbeson came out onto the porch, and said, "Sweetheart, you're not going anywhere. Buck, she's not to have the use of that rig. Sanchez, carry her bags into the house."

Helen looked from one to the other, hardly able to believe that they would dare hold her there against her will. But she saw that it was so.

CHAPTER SIXTEEN

By noon, Janet was in such a state of nerves that she felt quite ill. She hadn't slept at all during the night. She'd gone about her morning household chores after Helen's departure in such a temper that everything went wrong. A batch of bread turned out badly and a stew she was making for Ben's dinner boiled over and made a mess of her stove. Setting the table, she dropped and broke a platter, then cut a finger in picking up the shards of china. Suddenly she found herself thinking desperately: I've got to get away from here!

She couldn't rid herself of the picture of Helen in Jim's arms. Of course, she herself had ended her affair with Jim—such an affair as it had been. In the beginning, upon learning that he owned a herd of cattle, she'd considered him a good catch. He'd struck her as a man bound to prosper, and at the time a man who would make a proper sort of husband. Marriage with Jim had seemed the way to secure her future, and she'd begun to daydream and see herself living as Helen lived at Crescent Ranch. For a brief time, it had seemed that Jim Bannister would one day have a ranch like Crescent. But then he'd turned out to be stubborn and impractical, unwilling to take her advice—and so he'd got deeper and deeper into trouble.

Her life with Ben was one long struggle, a constant worry, and for a little while she'd hoped to escape from it. She had to admit that she wasn't in love with Jim; indeed, she imagined herself to be too practical-minded to believe in love. To Janet's way of thinking, a woman married to better her lot—not merely to indulge in what she considered the dubious pleasures of the bedroom. However, having seen the love scene between Helen and Jim, she'd experienced a full measure of jealousy. It still infuriated her.

Actually, Jim wasn't the first man she'd lost. Back in Missouri three years ago, she'd set her cap for a prosperous livestock dealer, only to lose him when she tried to advise him in a business deal with a friend who was getting the better part of the bargain. Like Jim, the livestock dealer had been so impractical that he harmed himself. And when he married a common dancehall girl, she'd hated him as she hated Jim Bannister now.

Yes, she did hate Jim Bannister.

Sometimes she felt that she hated all men. This morning Ben had been complaining to her. He'd been in one of his low moods; in fact, he'd been more discouraged than usual. No date had been set for the election of representatives to the Territorial Council, and worse still, he was beginning to suspect that he had little chance of being elected when the election was held. Business at the store was off, too. The past week had been his poorest to date, and besides, a homesteader who had run up a bill of thirty dollars had left the Strip. She couldn't bear much more of her brother's whining.

With dinner ready and the table set, she went through the house to the store to tell him to come eat. She heard an angry voice when she opened the door to the storeroom, then saw that it belonged to the Crescent foreman, Matt Harbeson. His face was brick-red with rage, and he was saying, "If I find out you're lying, Maury, I'll break your damn neck!"

He saw Janet the instant she stepped into the store, and shouted to her, "You! Let's hear your story. I want to see if it holds with his. Where'd Mrs. Forbes meet Bannister last night?"

She walked toward him, without fear that he'd catch her and Ben with conflicting stories. They'd foreseen the possibility of someone questioning them about that meeting, and agreed on what they would say.

She said, "I don't know how Mrs. Forbes got word to him. I didn't even know she was to meet him until she asked me to go with her and we were on the way. We met at an old homesteader place a couple miles from town."

He eyed her sourly. "He must have said where he's holed up."

"If he did, I didn't hear," Janet told him. "I wasn't included in their conversation." She couldn't help but add, "After all, two people engaging in a love scene hardly want a third person listening to what they say."

Harbeson swore. "You poor fools, you should have got word to me that he was around here. I might have been able to pick up his trail—and you would have collected that bounty on him."

He gave them a final disgusted look, then slammed out of the store.

For perhaps a minute Ben was silent and sullen after the door closed. Then he said, "He's the fool. People don't betray a friend even for five thousand dollars."

"Friend?" Janet said. "How much of a friend is he, actually?"

"What—what do you mean?"

"Five thousand dollars is a lot of money."

He stared at her.

She said, "With that much money we leave this godforsaken place and get a fresh start where there's some hope of success." Her voice rose, shrill with a hint of hysteria. "He's hiding in the Faro Hills, south of his place at Boot Creek. He'll be watching tonight for Jubal Kane to bring him a message from that Forbes woman, and he'll expect Kane to ride directly south from the buildings."

"Jan, you don't want—"

"Do as you please," she said, and turned away.

She went into the living room, closing the door. She stood by the door until, several minutes later, she heard her brother leave the store. For a moment a panicky feeling engulfed her and she had the impulse to run after him. But she fought against it.

Jim Bannister and Pat Keough remained in hiding all that day, passing much of the time in discussing ways and means of using Jake Maugher as a witness against Matt Harbeson. They had decided to set out for Rawson Wells at nightfall. By riding hard, they could reach the outlaw hangout in three hours. They would obtain fresh horses from a ranch Keough knew about, and then he would go into the town and alert Will Langley while Bannister stayed with their mounts. Keough would toll Maugher outside the place, and they would seize him. Once in their hands, the hardcase would be made into a willing witness—"in one way or another," as Pat Keough put it.

Bannister no longer found it strange that Keough was siding him. A happy-go-lucky sort, Pat Keough lived from day to day and cherished no dreams of riches. He couldn't imagine himself possessing five thousand dollars, he'd told Bannister, and he wanted no part of it if it meant throwing another man to the wolves, as he called it. Keough's needs were simple: grub, whiskey, an occasional game of cards for low stakes, a woman once in a while. He could make enough money rustling to satisfy such needs. He didn't go so far to claim such a thing, but Bannister decided that he was no hardened criminal but merely another cowboy who'd turned a little wild.

They ate some of the grub from Bannister's saddlebags at sundown, then saddled their horses. They rode out as dusk thickened into night, heading down from the hills toward the grass flats of Boot Creek range. They were quartering down a slope when a horse stamped and switched somewhere nearby in the darkness.

The first warning came from Keough: "Watch it, Jim—Watch it!"

At the same instant two horsemen appeared below them, one shouting, "This way, Crescent! This way!" A gun flashed, the report a sharp blast of sound shattering the night's quiet. Bannister grabbed for his own gun, at the same time wheeling his horse about to reclimb the slope. As the bay labored upslope, he twisted in the saddle and fired twice at the shadowy shapes of the two Crescent men who were coming after him and Keough. A moment later he caught the drumming of hoofs as a group of riders came along at a hard run. Keough was climbing the slope too, but in the opposite direction, and before Bannister reached the crest he lost sight of Keough.

Another shot racketed, then several more in

quick succession. He heard one slug shriek, but no others came close, and in another few seconds he was over the crest of the ridge and out of sight of his pursuers. He altered his course, riding in the direction Keough had taken. He reached the end of the ridge abruptly and descended into a little valley, striking across it at a hard run. He reached the base of a sheer cliff and reined in. Half a dozen riders were coming down into the valley, but he remained where he was, holstering his revolver and easing his rifle from its boot, on the chance that the shadows were deep enough to hide him.

They went tearing by, a hundred yards from him, heading back through the valley. When they passed from sight, he rode away from the cliff and a few minutes later climbed a slope at the valley's opposite end. Somebody shouted in the distance, and the sound, carried to him on the wind, seemed to come from the ridge where he'd escaped their gunfire. A second voice answered, much nearer. He held the bay to a walk, halted it frequently to listen. He continued to hear distant shouts, and finally somebody whistled softly in signal.

He reined in and called, "Pat?"

"Yeah. Come on. We're in the clear."

They found a gap in the hills and were midway through it when a drumming of hoofs sounded behind them. They rode at an easy lope, coming out onto open range, feeling safe enough now, for they'd given their mounts a rest while the Crescent hands chased one way and another at a pace that must have tired their horses. They aimed toward Bannister's buildings, and shortly saw them ahead. The Crescent hands were coming along behind them, but no longer at a run. They reached the bluffs in another few minutes, but Keough said, "This way, this way," and forded the creek instead of turning through the gap that would take them into the open country beyond the rocky barrier. They plunged into a brush thicket, and through it until thoroughly screened. They heard the racket of the Crescent men a minute later, then could see them—eight of them—aiming toward the cut. They went jogging through there, unaware that their quarry was no longer fleeing ahead of them, and shortly the clatter of hoofs faded in the distance.

Keough lighted a match, held the flame to a cigarette he'd made while waiting. "That does it," he said. "We'll have clear sailing now. But you know something, bucko? Those hombres didn't run into us by chance. They were laying for you."

"Yeah. They knew I'd show up there tonight."

"How come?"

"I was supposed to meet a friend coming into the hills after dark."

"And he tipped them off, this friend?"

Bannister said, "I don't know," and worried about it.

There was a possibility that Matt Harbeson had caught onto Jubal Kane and forced him to talk. It didn't seem likely that the old man's absences from ranch headquarters had gone unnoticed. Or perhaps Helen had unwittingly given it away while talking to the company bigwig, Vorhees. He didn't know J. P. Vorhees; he had only Helen's word for it that the man was a fair-minded person, and it might be that she had confided in him only to have him talk to Harbeson. There was Janet, of course. She too had known that he'd be watching for Kane tonight, and she considered herself a woman scorned. If she'd been angry enough to want to hurt him . . . He shied away from thinking such a thing.

"It doesn't matter, anyway," he said. "It was a trap, but we sidestepped it."

"Yeah," said Pat Keough. "Let's get going, eh?"

At Crescent, Helen Forbes told herself over and over that it was fantastic. In this day and age, people were not held against their will. But it was happening to her. She was a prisoner in this house. And by now she should realize that anything could happen in No Man's Land.

The future of her plan to clear Jim Bannister and fix the guilt of Matt Harbeson had almost crushed her. Harbeson was far more clever than she'd imagined. He'd discredited her with Mr. Vorhees, stripped her of respectability, and now he was keeping her here so that she couldn't get in touch with Jim Bannister. Keeping her here too, in the absurd hope that she'd eventually tire of widowhood and look upon him as a way out of it. She felt outraged that Harbeson should imagine she'd ever regard him with favor. Still, she understood him. He wasn't a madman, but an inordinately vain and ambitious man determined to have what he wanted.

She'd remained all afternoon in the bedroom which had been hers during the year she and John lived at Crescent Ranch, and now it was nightfall. She'd eaten hardly any breakfast, being upset by Janet's attitude, and had taken neither dinner nor supper. She was becoming weak from hunger. She considered going down to the kitchen to make a cup of tea and find a bite of food, but that might bring her face to face with Mr. Vorhees. After what Harbeson had made the old gentleman believe about her, she didn't want to see him. It would be embarrassing to them both.

She hadn't lighted the lamp, but sat in the dark at a window and looked out upon the wide ranch-yard. She'd seen Harbeson ride out immediately after she came to the room, and seen him return after sundown. He'd stayed only long enough to eat supper in the cookshack, then had ridden out with some of the hands. They hadn't come back yet.

Jubal Kane was among those of the crew who remained at headquarters, she knew, and he was her one hope of escaping. Somehow she must talk with him, but she didn't know how to accomplish that. Undoubtedly Harbeson had given the others orders to watch her every move if she ventured outside the house.

At long last she heard Mr. Vorhees's slow step on the stairs and along the hall, and the closing of his bedroom door. She waited a few minutes, then lighted a small hand lamp. Carrying it, went down to the kitchen.

She was kindling a fire in the stove when she heard the beat of hoofs as a rider came tearing into the yard. She put the kettle on the stove to boil water, and then, as she got the teapot down from the cupboard, she heard someone come into the house. The thumping of boots against the plank flooring was loud and arrogant, and she knew, before the man appeared at the kitchen doorway, that it was Matt Harbeson.

He was sweated and dusty, and his heavy face wore a black scowl. He halted just inside the doorway and stared as though he hated her. She thought it possible that he did hate her, even when he wanted her most. She turned her back and took a canister from the cupboard. She went to the table and began to spoon tea from the box to the pot. He pulled a chair away from the table, spun it around, straddled it. He pushed his hat back off his forehead and folded his arms upon the back of the chair.

"He got away again," he said. "He's as hard to catch as an Indian, but I'll get him. He's out of hiding and in the open, and this time I'll run him to earth. Your lover, I mean."

Helen had made up her mind not to let him draw her into a conversation, but this so infuriated her that she whirled and cried, "I won't be slandered like this!" Without conscious thought, she flung the teapot at him.

Her aim was good, and though he ducked, the pot struck his left temple. It knocked off his hat, jolted him half off the chair. He jumped up, cursing and holding his hand to his temple. Then abruptly he laughed.

"That's better," he said. "I've been wondering for a long time if there's any fire in you. I was afraid you were all ice, sweetheart."

"If you talk to me like that again, I'll kill you! I swear it!"

"All right, all right."

"And get out of here!"

His amusement faded. "Not until I've had my say," he told her. He picked up the teapot, set it on the table, then retrieved his hat. "I want you to know that I've talked to the Maurys. I got the truth out of them."

211

"So you bullied them!"

"Didn't need to. Ben Maury got the story from his sister, and he figured on collecting that reward."

"I don't believe it."

"Suit yourself. But I can tell you why they decided to talk. Janet's riled up because Bannister dropped her for you. She wanted to pay him back for that. He—" Harbeson fell silent, seeing her eyes blaze with sudden fury. "Hold your horses," he said. "I'll not say anything you don't want to hear. I just wanted you to know that you've got no friends in these parts any more. None but Bannister, and he's done for. Like I said, he's out of hiding and on the run. My boys are out now spreading word, and by morning he won't know which way to turn, there'll be so many men gunning for him."

Helen was shaken, and showed it. "How could you," she said, "when you know he didn't kill John Forbes? Doesn't your conscience ever bother you?"

"I sleep sound, honey."

"Your familiarities are disgusting, Harbeson. I'm not a silly schoolgirl flattered by cheap endearments. I'm not stupid, either." She drew a deep breath like a person about to plunge into deep, dangerous waters. "I'm bright enough to know you hired someone to murder my husband."

Harbeson laughed uproariously. "I hired a

bushwhacker?" he said. "Sweetheart, you're as wrong as you can be!"

He grinned at her for a while, seeming genuinely amused, then turned and went out. He left Helen shaken by doubt. His denial had had no counterfeit ring, and in spite of herself she wondered if he'd spoken the truth. Was Jim Bannister the guilty man, after all? She didn't want to suspect him again. The very thought tormented her. And yet it had to be either Harbeson or Jim, and Harbeson had laughed so heartily. . . .

She stood there, hopelessly confused. And, yes, frightened too.

CHAPTER SEVENTEEN

Coming from the house, Harbeson lapsed into the sour mood that had gripped him since Bannister slipped out of the trap earlier tonight. He hadn't stretched the truth for Helen Forbes. In a matter of hours—or a day, at most—that Texan would be run to earth. But it angered him to know that the man had outwitted him once more, if only temporarily. His hatred of Bannister had increased enormously upon learning that Helen had had a meeting with him, and at the moment it was the biggest thing in his life—greater than his wanting the woman or his need to secure his hold on Crescent Ranch.

Ever since her talk with old Vorhees he'd had an idea that she suspected him of back-shooting Forbes, and it brought some measure of relief to know that she merely guessed he'd hired somebody to do the killing. So long as she accused him of hiring, he could make his denials without any danger of sounding like a liar.

He still had something to take care of, something he'd put off doing when he returned from Dalton after talking to Ben Maury. That damn Kane . . . He crossed the yard, entered the bunkhouse, halting inside the doorway while his murky gaze searched the hall-like room for the old man.

Four of the hands were seated at the table, playing poker with matches for stakes. One man, also at the table, was sewing a patch on a shirt. A couple lay in their bunks and another was shaving at the wall mirror. Harbeson strode the length of the narrow room, then returned to the table.

"Where's Jubal?"

Nobody answered at once, and finally the man sewing the patch said, "How the hell should we know?"

Harbeson swore.

Jubal Kane came in from outside. "Looking for me, Matt?"

"You're damn right I'm looking for you." Harbeson walked toward Kane, his big hands clenched. "Where you been? Out saddling a horse to go meet that bushwhacking Bannister again?"

A look of surprise crossed Kane's craggy face, then he straightened until most of the stoop was gone from his shoulders. "So you know, Matt?" he said mildly. "Well, I'll tell you why I met him and then—"

His failure to show even a trace of fear threw Harbeson into an explosive rage. He shouted, "You'll tell me nothing, you sneaky old bastard!" and drove a fist to Kane's face.

That blow would have downed an ordinary man in his prime. Jubal Kane reeled backwards but refused to drop. He stood swaying, dazed, blood trickling from the corner of his mouth. But the old man didn't drop.

Harbeson said, "Aiding and abetting a murderer! I'll show you!" He took a forward step, but froze as one of the poker players said, "Lay off, Matt. He's no match for you, an old mossyhorn like him."

Harbeson looked over his shoulder, glowering at Buck McClure. He said, "What's that?" as though unable to believe his own ears.

A puncher named Duane said, "You heard him, Matt. Lay off."

Harbeson remained like that, staring at the men at the table, taken by surprise. This was the first time since he'd founded Crescent Ranch that any of the crew had crossed him. He couldn't ignore a challenge like this. He sensed that every man in the room was on the verge of mutiny. He'd have a brawl on his hands if he gave Kane a roughing-up. For some reason they thought more of the old rannihan than they did for him.

He said, "You know what he's pulled?"

Buck said, "We can guess. We're not exactly stupid, even if we are forty-a-month cowpokes. Jubal ran errands for Mrs. Forbes, and she sent him to meet Bannister. All right. So he crossed you up. But you ain't giving him a beating. Me, I'm getting sick of this fool Bannister business. It should never have been started, anyway. There's no end to it, and there won't be any until somebody else gets killed—and I've got a hunch it won't be that Texan. Anyway, keep your paws off Jubal."

Harbeson said savagely, "I'm still ramrodding this outfit, Buck. You'd better remember that or you'll be collecting your time, like Jubal is in the morning." He turned back to Kane. "Tell old Vorhees to pay you off tomorrow, then get the hell off Crescent range."

He received his reward in the way the old man flinched. Loss of his job hurt Kane more than a beating. A good hand he might still be, despite his years, but he'd have a sweet time finding another outfit that would hire him. Feeling somewhat better, Harbeson left the bunkhouse. He halted outside the doorway, listening to the mutter of voices behind him. He had the best men in crew, the toughest hands, Sanchez and Sherry among them, out spreading the word through the Strip that Bannister was on the run; these inside were the ones without guts—or at least, with soft streaks. And to hell with them, Harbeson told himself. But he wasn't convinced. They were as hardcased as himself, in most ways. They stood up for Jubal only because he was old and they felt sorry for him. In anything else, they were his men.

Or were they? Buck had said he was sick of the Bannister business, and it might be that the others felt the same way. Harbeson took out a cigar he'd picked up in the ranch office yesterday when talking with old Vorhees; it had come from Forbes's humidor. Lighting it, Harbeson had a sudden inspiration.

There was a way to keep the crew from getting out of hand. He'd quit bunking and eating with them, and thus give them no further chance to take him for just a hired hand like themselves. He'd move over into the main house. Why shouldn't he? Forbes was gone, and one of these days Vorhees would go back East. Yeah. Tomorrow he'd move his gear into one of the bedrooms over there.

He was relishing this idea when a rig loomed out of the darkness and turned into the ranchyard. It was a two-horse buggy, and two men rode in it. The driver reined in over by the house.

Harbeson started toward the rig, calling out, "Who are you hombres?"

The driver said, "I'm Len Macklin from Rawson Wells. I've got Judge Bateman with me. He wants to talk with Matt Harbeson."

Harbeson reached the buggy. Ignoring the driver, he stared at Bateman. "What do you want, you fourflushing rumdum?"

The lawyer said, with a show of dignity, "Keep a civil tongue, my man. Tonight I'm as sober as the proverbial judge. As for my errand, I'm here on behalf of a client. Where, sir, can we talk in comfort—and strict privacy?"

Some sixth sense told Harbeson that Bateman's visit meant trouble. Bateman was an occasional heavy drinker, but if there was work to do, he could go for months without touching the stuff. Harbeson felt contempt for any man who lived out of a bottle, and Bateman had let whiskey drag him down from the practice of law to being a hanger-on in an outlaw nest. True, he was backing Bateman for the Territorial Council, but only because Bateman, hand-glove with the outlaws and the sporting crowd, was running against Ben Maury who wanted to over-run No Man's Land with homesteaders. The scheme to organize a government in the Neutral Strip had made little progress lately, and Harbeson hoped it would wither on the vine. Still, he knew somehow that Judge Bateman hadn't come to discuss politics.

"All right," he said. "Come over to the cook-shack."

He lighted the lamp there, and Bateman entered and seated himself on one of the benches at the long table. The man had told the truth; he was sober, or nearly so. He'd slicked himself up a bit: shaved his florid, puffy face and got his hair trimmed. He'd brushed his threadbare suit, polished his worn shoes, got hold of a new hat. Harbeson stood on the opposite side of the table, one foot on the bench and one arm resting on his knee.

"Let's have it, Judge."

"I have a client—"

"So you said. You have a client, and now you're a lawyer again."

Bateman harrumphed, annoyed. "Your interruptions are pointless, sir," he said. "My client, who wishes to remain anonymous, retained me to discuss a matter of importance with you. The matter concerns the murder of one, John Forbes."

Harbeson stiffened, but said nothing.

Bateman continued, "It seems that a party named Bannister is a suspect in the murder of Forbes. However, Bannister is wrongly suspected. My client was a witness to the murder and, after long deliberation, he has decided that he is doing less than his duty in remaining silent. His decision is to testify before any interested persons, and his testimony will of course clear Bannister."

Harbeson's face suddenly beaded with sweat, and his breathing hurried. He remembered the horseman he'd seen immediately after he shot John Forbes. He knew who that horseman had been.

He said, "So your client is Jake Maugher."

"I didn't say so, sir."

"Quit the fancy talk," Harbeson said. "What's Jake want?"

"The reward for Bannister is five thousand dollars?"

"You know it is."

Bateman nodded. "I merely wanted it verified. Now my client doesn't want to see a miscarriage of justice. He feels that the Crescent Cattle Company would want to know that Bannister is not the murderer and therefore should be willing to pay the same reward for the name of the man who is guilty. Would the Crescent Cattle Company pay the reward in such a case, Harbeson?"

A sickly chill took hold of Matt Harbeson. He stared at the lawyer in silence, wondering how much Jake Maugher had told Bateman. He could see a certain slyness in the man's bloodshot eyes, and was sure he knew it all.

He said thickly, "If your client could talk to the right person, the company would probably pay."

"My client is aware that an officer of the company is now here at Crescent."

"Yeah. But just how does he figure on getting to that officer of the company? The man he thinks is the murderer may bushwhack him before he gets here."

Bateman nodded. "He has considered that possibility. He has two courses open to him. One, he can get in touch with the company officer— Mr. J. P. Vorhees, I believe the gentleman's name is—when he leaves Crescent Ranch to return East. Two, he can make public knowledge of the fact that he witnessed the murder—and thus the name of the murderer will reach the ears of Mr. Vorhees."

"Cute," Harbeson said. "Jake's got it all figured out. How much does he want, Judge?"

"The figure he mentioned was ten thousand dollars."

"He's crazy!"

"Hardly. If it's worth five thousand to the Crescent Cattle Company to know who actually murdered Forbes, it should be worth twice that to you—to keep the company from learning it."

Harbeson swore under his breath. But it was out in the open now, and he could find a way to deal with these blackmailers. He said, "Just where am I to get hold of that much money? Are you and Jake forgetting that I'm only ranch boss here at Crescent, working for wages?"

"We're not forgetting that you're a stockholder in the Crescent Cattle Company," Bateman said. "And it's a prosperous company that no doubt is paying large dividends."

"I can't raise one half ten thousand."

"My client thinks otherwise."

"Your client is a damn fool so far as I'm concerned. Maybe you'd better go tell him to go jump through a hoop, for me."

Bateman looked at him with surprise. "Is that your final word, Harbeson?"

Matt Harbeson felt like grabbing Bateman and throwing him bodily from the cookshack. But caution came to him. Jake Maugher and his fraud of a lawyer had him over a barrel, and he needed to go easy until he found a way to deal with them, short of paying for their silence. He felt like a man caught in quicksand. Ever since he'd first seen that damn Jim Bannister, he'd sunk deeper and deeper into trouble. Still, it wouldn't be long until Bannister was trapped, and then he'd be able to handle everything else. He'd have to buy a little time now, though.

"All right," Harbeson said. "You and Jake keep your mouths shut. I'll pay you what I can."

A gleam showed in Bateman's bloodshot eyes. "How much on account?" he said. "My client doesn't expect you to have that much cash on hand, of course. But he does count on my returning with at least a thousand."

"The best I can do tonight is five hundred."

"That's rather disappointing."

"Take it or leave it."

"I'll take it," Judge Bateman said. "And I'll return in a week for more."

Harbeson nodded, thinking that in a week he'd find a way out of this mess. Bateman and Jake could be paid off with lead, if need be.

The lawyer must have read his thoughts. He said, "My client instructed me to tell you that he's signed a deposition stating the facts of the Forbes murder, and placed it in safe hands. If anything should happen to him, such as a fatal accident, the document will be made public.

You understand the necessity of that, of course?"

"Yeah," Harbeson said thickly. "Of course."

Three hours of fast travel brought Jim Bannister and Pat Keough to a ranch within a mile of Rawson Wells. Out behind the ranch buildings was a fenced meadow holding a large number of horses, and Keough said, "Wait for me over at the gate."

Bannister rode on, and behind him Keough sang out, "Hey, Bart! Open up, man, you've got visitors!" By the time Bannister reined in by the meadow gate, a light bloomed within the sod house. Five minutes later Keough came along and dumped a saddle to the ground.

"That'll be for the horse we give Jake," he said. "Open the gate, bucko."

They rode into the meadow and by the light of the moon each picked out and roped a fresh mount. After shifting his saddle to the borrowed horse, Bannister dropped his loop on another animal and led it outside the fence. Keough saddled it with the rigging he'd got from the rancher, then took it in tow when they rode on toward Rawson Wells.

Keough chuckled. "Know whose place that is?"

"No."

"Bart Maugher's. Bart's a brother to Jake. Some joke on those two, eh?"

Bannister laughed. "Anyway, Jake shouldn't complain about riding one of his brother's broncs."

They saw the lights of Rawson Wells ahead, but didn't aim directly toward the place. Keough led the way to a broad hollow west of town. It was littered with rocks and brush. At the edge of the hollow, Keough gave Bannister the reins of the spare horse.

"I'll get back with Will Langley and Jake as soon as I can make it," he said. "If I don't show up by an hour before dawn, you'll know something went wrong."

"And if something goes wrong?"

"You'd better hightail it, in that case."

"All right," Bannister said. "Luck, Pat."

He watched Keough ride toward the town, it occurring to him then that if this scheme to seize Jake Maugher misfired, he'd be in a tight corner. He didn't dare return to the Faro Hills, now that Harbeson knew he'd been hiding there all along. The Crescent boss would almost certainly take his entire crew into the Faros and fine-comb them again, against his returning there. And in a country with as few hills and stretches of broken country as No Man's Land, it would be difficult to find another safe hideout. He faced the disheartening fact that unless he got hold of Jake Maugher and forced the hardcase to clear him, he was done for. He'd have no choice but to run for it, to run for his life. It had come to that, and there was no logic in thinking otherwise. Bannister rode down into the hollow. He dismounted, built a smoke and tried to convince himself that things would work out.

He was close enough to the town to hear its rowdy sounds. Evidently Rawson Wells stayed as much awake by night as by day. He heard the music of a piano and a fiddle, loud voices, a woman's shrill laughter. A bunch of riders left the place at a hard run, yelling at the top of their lungs and shooting off their guns. Two men shouted in a bitter argument. Hoofs pounded as a rider came in from the south at a hard run. Bannister finished his cigarette, rolled and lighted another. The waiting was hard.

More than an hour passed before he heard Keough returning. The rustler whistled in signal, then rode down the hollow. Will Langley was with him, but not Jake Maugher. Bannister's disappointment was so keen that he greeted Langley with only a brief handshake.

Then he said, "No luck, Pat?"

"None at all," Keough said. "Jake left town this afternoon. Will saw him go. He had his bedroll tied behind his saddle, and he rode north toward the Kansas line. I asked around the place, but nobody knew where Jake was headed. While I was there a Crescent hand came riding in. You know Sanchez?"

"I know him."

"Well, he's spreading word that you're out of your hideout and in the open," Keough said. "He's telling the boys they should go gunning for you again, because now that you're on the run you'll be easy game. He's talking up that five-thousand-dollar reward real big, and you can count on it that a lot of them will swallow the bait. Jim-boy, you're in trouble. The rest of the Crescent hands are probably carrying the word in other directions, and by morning the whole Strip will be stirred up again. We've got to find you a safe place to hole up."

Bannister nodded, but said, "What time this afternoon did Jake leave, Will?"

"About four o'clock," Langley said. "It seems queer, his pulling out for Kansas when we know he's aiming to blackmail Matt Harbeson." He glanced at Keough. "Maybe he was pulling a windy with that talk about seeing Harbeson bushwhack Forbes."

Keough shook his head. "Jake ain't no joker."

"No," Bannister said, "he's a smart hombre. And being smart, he wouldn't go to Harbeson, himself. He'd send somebody, and then make himself scarce so Harbeson couldn't shut his mouth with a couple of forty-five slugs. It could be he's just getting in touch with Harbeson through a friend, while he goes up to Kansas so Harbeson can't get at him."

"Sounds reasonable," Keough said. "Jake wouldn't dare let Harbeson get at him."

Langley said, "I've got it. Jake was riding herd on a drunk named Judge Bateman for the past couple of days. He sobered the judge up, and kept him sober. Today, just before Jake left, he put Bateman in a buggy driven by a man named Macklin and they headed south. They could have been headed for Crescent Ranch. If Jake wanted a man who could talk up to Harbeson, it would be the judge. We could catch him on his way back from Crescent and make him tell us where Jake went."

"He won't know," Bannister said. "Jake would be afraid that Harbeson might force Bateman to tell it."

"Still," Keough said, "the judge has to know how to get in touch with Jake. Here's what we'll do, Jim. We'll have a jug of rotgut along when we meet up with Bateman. He'll be mighty thirsty by then. We'll get him likkered up, then pump him. The trouble is, we may not meet up with him until tomorrow, and then the manhunt will be on again. We've got to find you a hideout."

"Don't bother about me," Bannister said. "I'm going after Jake. Maybe I can pick up his trail. And even if I don't, I'll be safer up in Kansas than here in No Man's Land while the manhunt's on."

He swung into the saddle. "Take care of that

spare horse, Pat," he said. "And if you get anything out of the judge, look for me up there. What's the nearest town?"

"Fenton."

"Look for me at Fenton."

Will Langley said, "Watch your step there, Jim. Folks there will have heard about that bounty offer, and five thousand dollars is as big in some parts of Kansas as it is in the Strip."

Keough said, "I just remembered something. Jake was crazy about a dancehall girl named Lil Shannon. About a week ago she left Rawson Wells to go to Fenton. It might pay you to look her up. If we can't get anything out of Judge Bateman, you may get something out of Lil."

Bannister wheeled his horse about and rode from the hollow. With flat country ahead of him, he lifted it to a lope. Jake Maugher had a seven- or eight-hour start, but likely he wasn't traveling fast. By morning, Bannister told himself, Maugher wouldn't have much of a lead left.

The only sound in the night was the beat of hoofs and creak of saddle leather.

CHAPTER EIGHTEEN

In Kansas, people built with plank instead of sod. But they didn't paint their buildings and houses, and consequently Fenton was as much of an eyesore as Dalton or any settlement in No Man's Land.

Bannister rode into the town just before nightfall.

He could have arrived there much earlier, but he'd decided that it would be safer to wait until darkness came. By daylight, the townspeople would get too good a look at him. They wouldn't know him by sight, of course, but Crescent just might have circulated a good description of him. Also, Jake Maugher might not spot him at night. He'd spent part of the day at a German homesteader place, fed by the sodbuster's wife and permitted to sleep in the barn. The couple had spoken hardly any English, and so they couldn't know he was a man with a price on his head. They'd been grateful for the dollar he paid them for the meal.

He'd visited Fenton before, on his trip to Kansas a year ago. It was on the railroad, a small but bustling place, and he went directly to McDade's livery barn, near the station, to stable his horse. It was a sorrel gelding in the Running M iron, and the hostler recognized the brand. "Friend of Bart Maugher's are you?"

"Yeah," Bannister said easily. "You know Bart?"

The hostler grinned. "Sure. The boss, McDade, buys horses from him now and then. Good, cheap horses."

Bannister returned the grin, because Bart Maugher dealt in stolen horse. Then he said, "You know Jake too?"

"Sure."

"He's been in today?"

"Yeah. Left his horse early this morning."

"He's still in town, then?"

"Nope. He hired a buckboard and team this afternoon, and drove out."

"Know where he headed?"

The hostler said, "Nope," and began to eye Bannister with curiosity, if not suspicion.

Bannister tried a silver dollar on him, saying, "Bart sent me with a message for Jake. It's important for me to deliver it."

The dollar went into the hostler's pocket, and he said, "Jake didn't say where he was headed, mister. He drove into town, and about an hour later I saw him pass on his way out of town. He had a woman with him, one of those fancy women from the deadfalls. He had some luggage tied in back of the buckboard. Hers, I guess. They crossed the tracks and headed out the north road."

"What's north, friend?"

"Some ranches, a bunch of settler places, and beyond them a lot of nothing."

Bannister said, "Well, thanks," and left the stable.

Hungry again, he went into a place called the Trail Cafe and had ham and eggs, coffee and a wedge of apple pie. The place was fairly crowded. Nobody paid any attention to him, but he heard two men at the counter talking about the five-thousand-dollar reward being offered for some killer down in the Strip. One man said he'd sure as shooting like to collect that kind of a bounty, and the conversation made Bannister edgy.

He bought a cigar when he paid for his meal, then stood on the plank sidewalk outside the cafe and lighted it. As he smoked, his mind kept busy. Pat Keough had said that Jake Maugher was crazy about a gay lady by the name of Lil Shannon who had come to Fenton about a week ago. Apparently Jake had sent Lil here ahead of him, planning to pick her up and take her elsewhere.

Jake had wanted company while hiding out beyond Matt Harbeson's reach. Somehow, Bannister told himself, he had to find out where Jake was hiding, and at the moment hadn't any idea of how to go about it.

There was one dancehall on the main street, connected with the Alhambra Saloon, and another, a cheaper place, over in the Front Street red light district. Bannister went to the Alhambra. It was too early in the evening for the dancehall to draw customers, but he found a couple of the girls sitting in the barroom. As he'd expected, one gave him an inviting smile and he joined her. He bought two rounds of drinks, and finally the chance came to ask her if she knew a girl named Lil Shannon.

"I know them all," she told him. "None of them calls herself by that monicker."

"Would you know her if she just came to town about a week ago?"

"Maybe not. But now that I think about it, I remember hearing that there's a new one over at Hilda's Place on Front Street."

"Thanks. I'll go around there."

"What's your hurry, handsome?" the girl said. "Ain't I good company?"

"Sure, you are," Bannister said. "I'll probably be back later."

He left the Alhambra and set out for Hilda's Place. Front Street faced the railroad tracks, and consisted of a short row of parlor houses and cribs with Hilda's Place midway along it. Here too, business was slow, and three women in succession solicited Bannister before he turned in under the crudely painted but gaudy red and yellow sign that read: *Hilda's Place—Girls & Drinks—Sporting Gentlemen Welcome.*

There was a bar at one side of the narrow

room, a row of tables at the other, and a space for dancing at the rear. Nobody was dancing, and the piano player, lonely in the far corner, played dispiritedly. In the corner opposite the piano a stairway led to the second floor, and a couple of girls sat talking on a lower step. Three men drank at the bar, one with a girl. A man in a checkered suit and a hard hat, obviously a drummer, sat at a table with another girl. A woman sat on a high stool at the end of the bar near the door, presiding over the till. She was middle-aged, a big woman in a green velvet dress that left her hefty arms, shoulders and much of her bosom bare. Her hair was hennaed. She bestowed a welcoming smile on Bannister, and it revealed a diamond set into each of two of her front teeth. This must be Hilda, and a frightening lot of woman she was. Bannister realized that if she knew where Lil Shannon had gone it would cost him more than he could afford to get her to talk. Still, he had so much at stake that it hardly mattered if he went broke.

"Greetings, stranger," the woman said. "Welcome to Hilda's. What'll your pleasure be this evening?"

"A drink to start with," he said, and turned to the bartender. "Set them up for everybody, friend. I'm buying this round."

Hilda made a furtive signal, and one of the girls on the stairs came and linked her arm with Bannister's. He looked at her, smiled, and decided immediately that he might learn more from her than from the formidable proprietress. She was a little thing, barely reaching to his shoulder, a bleached blonde and pretty enough. She returned the smile in a mechanical fashion.

"Want to dance with Rita, handsome?"

"Later. Let's take a table for a while."

She hugged his arm. "Whatever you say."

He paid for the first round of drinks, then told the bartender to serve him and the girl another at the table. He led her to the one farthest back through the room so that he had her well away from Hilda. When their drinks came, he lifted his and said, smiling, "Here's to us, honey." His was whiskey, and he knew that hers was merely cold tea or some other innocuous drink, though he paid the same price for each. Several more customers came into the place, making it noisier. The professor played on, but still nobody danced.

Bannister said, "All the girls here now?"

Rita looked around. "All but one. She's upstairs—busy. Why do you want to know?"

"I was looking for a girl I know."

"It's Lou Marvin who's not here."

Bannister shook his head. "That's not the one," he said. He'd never been much of a hand at lying, but it seemed that a man could do most anything well when he was desperate. "I knew this girl down in No Man's Land. She left there about a week ago, and I heard she was working here. Her name's Lil Shannon."

"Oh, her."

"She's not here?"

"No, she left this afternoon," Rita said. "But why bother about her? There's nothing wrong with me, is there?"

The bartender came without being called and set fresh drinks on the table. Bannister paid for them, but didn't touch his. Three shots within less than ten minutes were too many when he had to keep his wits about him. He took out tobacco sack and papers and started making a cigarette. Rita was still waiting for his answer, and, looking her over, he found nothing wrong with her. She was not small where it mattered. Her breasts filled the bodice of her red dress so fully they strained the seams. She leaned toward him, so he could have no doubt about her attractions.

"Dance now?"

"The truth is, I can't dance."

"I could teach you."

"I don't think I want to learn, honey. It's something I won't have much use for, after I leave here."

"Want to go where we can be alone?"

"All right."

"Buy a bottle. It'll be all right with Hilda if we go upstairs."

He rose with her, then went to the bar and

bought a bottle of whiskey. Hilda beamed on him as he paid. He followed Rita to the stairs, and as he climbed he watched the undulating of her backside just ahead of him. She wasn't small there, either. She led him into a cubby-hole of a room furnished with a bed, a washstand, a chair, and little else. Rita got glasses and eyed him curiously.

"Well, pull the cork, why don't you?"

He set the bottle on the washstand. "Rita—"

"What's the matter? Don't you want a party?"

"How much do you want?"

"Oh, so that's it. You're a piker, are you?"

He took a five dollar gold piece from his pocket and laid it beside the bottle. He said, "I need a shave. I smell of horses and my own sweat. I haven't changed clothes in I don't know how long. I doubt if having me here is any pleasure for you."

She frowned. "You're a queer one."

"Do you know where Lil Shannon went, Rita?"

"So that's it. You've got a yen for her and nobody else will do."

"It's not that," he said. "This is—well, something else. I've got to find the man she went off with. I don't care a damn about her, except that maybe I can find him through her. It's important, Rita."

"Man, you are worked up," she said, in an altered tone. "This man—Maugher is his name—

came here and they had a big argument. Lil wasn't anxious to go with him, but he kept telling her he'd come into some big money—or was about to. I heard it, because Lil was in the next room and you can hear a whisper through these walls. Lil finally agreed to go with him and—well, they cleared out."

"Did they mention where they were going?"

"Yes. He told her they wouldn't go far, only about seven miles north of Fenton to Red Sorensen's ranch. He said she could come to town any time she wanted."

Bannister patted her shoulder. "Thanks, honey," he said. "You've saved my life—and I'm not fooling."

He turned to the door, then faced about when she said, "Wait a second." She came to him, stood on her toes, touched her lips to his. "Come back sometime, won't you?"

"You bet," he said, and went out.

As he descended the stairs he wondered why he hadn't stayed. Another hour wouldn't have mattered, since he now knew where to find Jake Maugher. But he didn't need to puzzle over it for long. He hadn't wanted Rita because of Helen Forbes, whom he could never have.

From Hilda's Place, he went to McDade's Livery Stable. And for another silver dollar, the hostler gave him exact directions to Sorensen's ranch.

CHAPTER NINETEEN

Sorensen's place was easy to locate. Bannister kept to the north road until it forded a creek, then turned west along the stream. The buildings were no more than half a mile from the road—a house, a barn and some sheds, all of plank and with tarpaper roofs. The windows of the house glowed with light. Bannister slow-walked his horse in behind the barn and dismounted. He had no idea how many men the house held, and he realized it hardly mattered. He had to take Jake Maugher, whatever the odds. He couldn't return to No Man's Land without him.

He walked from behind the barn with his gun in his hand, and headed toward the house. He found the door slightly ajar. He heard a man say, "Come on, Jake, drink up!" and laugh uproariously.

Then a woman said, "Jake, you fool, he's trying to drink you under the table!"

He pushed the door wide open and stepped into the room.

Three people sat at a plank table, in the center of which stood a jug. Jake Maugher was in the act of drinking from a tin cup under the amused gaze of a giant red-haired man. Jake went on drinking, but the other man and the woman stared at Bannister, startled.

The woman said, "Who's this, Red?"

"Don't know," Red Sorensen said. He cocked an inquiring eye at the gun. "Is that thing loaded, stranger?"

Bannister closed the door and stood with his back to it. Jake Maugher drained his cup and set it down. He looked stupidly at Bannister. He was very drunk.

Bannister said, "It's loaded, Red, so take it easy. I want no trouble with you. I've come for Jake."

Jake peered at Bannister, his whiskey-befogged brain beginning to wonder. "Who're you?" he muttered. "Why'd you come after me, huh?"

Bannister ignored him. Jake wasn't wearing his gun, and he couldn't have made use of one, anyway. However, Sorensen was sober enough, and, though also unarmed, he looked dangerous. A coarsely handsome man, he seemed to have shaved within the past hour or two. He wore a clean shirt, and had his red hair slicked down. Compared to the grubby-looking Jake Maugher, he was almost a dude. After a moment of staring at Bannister, Sorensen laid his hands palm-down on the table to show that he wasn't dealing himself in on this game.

"So you've come for Jake," he said. "All right. But what now?"

"I'm taking him on a little trip."

"No killing, then?"

"No killing," Bannister said. "He's worth too much to me alive."

The woman said, "You the man Jake's supposed to collect all that money from?" She didn't wait for a reply, but went on, "He didn't expect you so soon. He said the money wouldn't come for two, three days."

A tin cup stood before her on the table, and she had been drinking from it. Her cheeks were flushed from the whiskey and her eyes unnaturally bright, but she was far from being as drunk as Jake. A dark blonde, on the buxom side, she wore slippers and a wrapper and nothing else.

Sorensen said suddenly, "You're not taking her?"

"No."

"All right, then."

Bannister understood. Whatever the deal between Jake and the big man, it was less important to Sorensen than the woman. He'd decided that he wanted her, and he'd been trying to drink Jake into insensibility so he could have her. Bannister began to think his luck had changed. This looked to be easier than he'd dared hope.

Jake blurted out, "It's the Texan!" Spasms of mingled fear and hate twisted his face. He heaved out of his chair, upsetting it. Then the rotgut whiskey got him. He fell forward onto the table, rolled off it to the floor, and lay sprawled in a drunken stupor.

"What Texan?" Sorensen asked, of nobody.

The woman said, "Who cares? The world's full of Texans. Take it from me."

Sorensen looked at her, then at Jake. He smiled slyly and said, "All right, Texan. He's yours to take. But how are you taking him? You'll never get him on a horse."

"With your help, I will."

"What makes you think I'm going to help?"

"You want to be rid of him. You've decided three makes a crowd."

Sorensen laughed. "You're a sharp one, Texas. Jake promised me a hundred dollars to put him up for a couple weeks, but I can get along without the money. Say the word, and I'll take him outside and put him on a horse."

"It's said, Red."

Sorensen rose. He bent over the unconscious Jake. He caught hold of him, jerked him upright and took him over his shoulder as he might have taken a sack of grain. Jake was no burden at all for him. He turned toward the door, rumpling the woman's hair as he passed her.

"I'll be back, Lil baby."

Bannister followed him outside, thinking that his luck had indeed changed.

Taking no chances, he kept his gun ready during the fifteen minutes it took Sorensen to rope a horse in his corral, saddle it, and then get Jake on its back. On Bannister's orders, Sorensen tied

Jake's wrists to the pommel so that he wouldn't fall from the saddle. Finally he stepped back, eyeing Bannister curiously.

"What's it all about, anyway, Texas?"

"Nothing that concerns you, Red."

"Well, luck to you."

Bannister said, "Thanks," and holstered his gun. He led Jake's horse around behind the barn and mounted his own sorrel. Then, leading Jake's mount, he set out at a lope through the darkness. Glancing back, he saw Red Sorensen entering the house. The door closed behind the man.

Bannister swung wide of Fenton, then aimed for the German's homestead. He arrived there with a sober but sick Jake Maugher shortly after daybreak, and found the farmer milking his cow in the little barn. By using the simplest of words and much sign language, plus a five-dollar gold piece, Bannister made a deal with the man for meals and the use of his barn during the day. The German looked worried when he saw that Bannister had Jake tied to his horse, but he shrugged and went about his chores. He came out ahead on the deal, for Jake refused to eat and only took a cup of coffee at supper.

They left the place at dusk, and this time Bannister let his prisoner have his hands free to guide his horse. But he told him, "No tricks, Jake. Try anything and I'll use a gun on you.

I'm not going to fool around any with you."

They headed southeast toward a huge blood-red moon that hung barely above the horizon. Bannister kept Jake ahead of him, and he set the pace, alternating between a lope and a fast walk and prodding the Maugher with a "Come on, come on," when he held back. About an hour after nightfall, Jake got his nerve back and grew rebellious.

"What the hell do you think this will get you, Bannister?"

"As if you don't know, friend."

"Suppose I tell you I'll not be scared into anything?"

"Don't waste your breath saying it," Bannister told him.

Heading southeast, he avoided the outlaw town of Rawson Wells and the section surrounding it. With luck, he would elude anybody out man-hunting him from there. On the other hand, he was going miles out of his way, since his destination was Crescent Ranch and the shortest route to its headquarters went through the Wells. By this detour, he wouldn't reach Crescent until daylight, and thus he would run the risk of being seen by Harbeson or some of his men on his way in. If they did spot him, he'd have to fight against such odds that there would be no chance of coming out of it alive. To reach the Crescent ranch house and J. P. Vorhees safely, he needed the cover of darkness and would have to delay his arrival there until tomorrow night. That meant spending a day in the open, at the risk of being spotted by bounty-hunters—which also would involve him in a fight against odds, unless he could find a hideout.

He could think of only one place where he might be safe.

The Maurys' house.

He headed toward Dalton.

He called a halt in the small hours of the morning to rest the horses. He dismounted and ordered Jake to get down. He rolled a cigarette, then offered the makings to his prisoner. Jake refused them with a muttered oath. Bannister lighted up and dragged the smoke deep into his lungs. He'd slept little during the day; he couldn't remember when he'd had a full night's rest. He felt tired to the core, and a little low in spirit. He was gambling on getting past the bounty-hunters scattered throughout No Man's Land, on dodging Matt Harbeson and the Crescent crew, and on being able to force Jake Maugher to talk. He wondered if he wasn't a prize fool.

He smoked his cigarette short, dropped it and ground it beneath his boot. He swung to the sorrel's saddle and said, "Let's go, Jake." Jake obeyed sullenly, then swung his horse about so that he faced Bannister.

"Look, I want to know. Where are you taking me?"

"To Crescent, tomorrow night."

"You loco? You'll get us both killed."

"That's something to worry about, I admit. Still, that's where we're going."

"It'll do you no good, even if Harbeson doesn't kill us."

"It'll do me plenty of good. You're going to talk to that Crescent Cattle Company bigwig," Bannister said. "You're going to tell him who killed John Forbes."

"And if I don't?"

"Why, in that case, friend, I'm going to throw you to the wolves," Bannister said. "The way I look at it, Matt Harbeson probably wants you more than he wants me—since you tried to blackmail him through Judge Bateman." He saw Jake Maugher wince, and knew he'd hit upon the one thing that would throw a scare into him. He cinched it by adding, "You'll talk to Vorhees, friend, or I'll give you to Harbeson—even if I've got to risk my own neck to do it. Now get going!"

Jake went.

They reached Dalton at dawn, going to the barn behind the Maurys' building. They off-saddled the horses, and Jake, on Bannister's orders, carried water for them from the pump outside Janet's kitchen door. There was a bale of hay for the horse Ben kept in the barn, and Jake forked some of it loose for their animals. Then he spread some gunny-sacks in a corner and stretched out on them, one arm covering his eyes. He lay there pitying himself, Bannister supposed. Bannister had closed the door except for an inch-wide crack, and he hunkered down by it smoking a cigarette and listening for sounds which would tell him that the Maurys were up and about. Jake and he would need at least one meal today, and he hoped Janet wouldn't mind feeding them. He realized that he wouldn't be too welcome since he'd angered the girl by favoring Helen Forbes instead of her. But he didn't believe she would be so heartless as to refuse him a meal.

Finally he heard the screech of the pump, and peered through the opening. He saw Ben Maury working the handle. The merchant washed up, then pumped water into a pail and carried it inside. Next Bannister noticed smoke beginning to puff from the pipe chimney, showing that Janet had kindled a breakfast fire. He rose and prodded Jake with the toe of his boot.

"Come on," he said. "We'll bum breakfast."

Jake rose obediently, mechanically. The threat of turning him over to Matt Harbeson had worked wonders. They left the barn and crossed to the house. The kitchen door stood open. Ben was knotting his string tie as they entered, and Janet stood at the stove. Ben froze, a stricken look on his face. An oddly guilty look, it seemed to Jim Bannister. Janet turned, showing only a mild surprise when her gaze touched Jake Maugher. Then, upon seeing Bannister, she dropped the coffee pot and screamed.

Seeing the girl cover her face with her hands, Bannister was startled and bewildered. Then he understood. Janet had been the one who told Matt Harbeson he was hiding in the Faro Hills. Because of Janet, he and Pat Keough had ridden into a gun-trap the night they left the hills.

Janet began to sob, and he felt sick at heart.

CHAPTER TWENTY

He went to her and slipped his arm about her. "Forget it, Jan," he said. "I have."

She pressed her face against his shoulder. "I can't. I'll never forgive myself."

"It was done in anger. I know that."

"Yes, but—"

"Who doesn't do crazy things in anger?" he said; and then; "I want you and Ben to hear this." He jabbed his finger at Jake Maugher. "Say your piece, Jake."

Jake looked stubborn, at first, but finally he shrugged and said, "Matt Harbeson killed John Forbes. I was nearby. I heard the shot and saw Forbes fall from his buckboard. I Injunned around for a look at the killer. It was Matt Harbeson who came from the Graveyard, and there was nobody else around. So it had to be him that killed Forbes."

Ben and Janet were in an agony of embarrassment.

Bannister said, "I'm taking Jake to Crescent Ranch tonight and have him tell J. P. Vorhees. But I'm still in danger and I've got to hide today. If you'll put up with us until tonight—"

Ben Maury nodded, and Janet said, "It's the least we can do for you, Jim." She used the corner

249

of her apron to wipe away tears. "If I could only make it up to you, really make it up to you. And to Jubal Kane. I feel so guilty about him."

"What about Jubal?"

"He lost his job because of my—my having Ben talk to Matt Harbeson."

"Where is he now?"

"He was here in town yesterday."

Bannister looked at Ben Maury. "If he's still around, I'd like to see him," he said. "How about hunting him up after breakfast?"

Maury agreed, and shortly after they'd eaten and Bannister had taken Jake back to the barn, Jubal Kane arrived.

A smile softened Kane's craggy face.

"You sure lead a charmed life, bucko," he said. "Harbeson has everybody gunning for you again, and here you are—still safe and sound."

"And I've got him where I want him, Jubal."

"Ah?"

"Jake here witnessed the Forbes murder."

Kane grinned at Jake Maugher, his eyes bright with a lively interest. "Now, ain't that something?" he said. "But it's no surprise to me that Harbeson's the man. I had a hunch he bushwhacked Forbes. But how are you going to make use of knowing that? There's no law to go to, remember. Harbeson will laugh in your face. Worse than that, he'll fix the pair of you—for keeps."

250

"He'll try, maybe," Bannister said. "But not until after I've seen Vorhees. I'll queer him with the Crescent Cattle Company, at least. Unless Vorhees is the sort that can stomach a killer."

"Old Mr. Vorhees is all right," Kane said. "He'll kick Harbeson off Crescent Ranch, sure. And that's something I want to see. I'll ride with you tonight, bucko. I've got a hunch you may need a friend."

"Glad to have you along, Jubal."

"Too bad you don't have some more friends."

"I've got a couple, but I don't know where they are right now."

"Who are they? Maybe I can find them for you."

"Will Langley, my hired hand," Bannister said. "Pat Keough, the rustler." He shook his head. "I doubt if you can find them. I went up to Kansas after Jake, and they were to follow me. I left there sooner than I'd expected, so I missed them. You could ride over to Rawson Wells, on the chance that they either didn't go up there or came back already."

Kane nodded. "I'll ride over there. Where will I meet you tonight?"

"At Crescent headquarters," Bannister told him. "I'll leave here at full dark. By moving fast, I'll get there in about three hours. Meet me out behind the ranch house. We'll go in through the kitchen."

Kane turned to go, but he faced about at the door. "Don't get the idea Harbeson will call it quits without a showdown. He's apt to turn all hell loose when old Vorhees calls him in and gives him the bad news. You've got to understand Matt Harbeson, Bannister. Crescent Ranch is everything to him and he'll fight to keep it."

"Yeah," Bannister said. "And that's his weak spot."

"How do you figure that?"

"He'll go too far to hold onto Crescent," Bannister said. "And then somebody will have to kill him." He gave Jubal Kane a searching look. "That's in your mind, isn't it? That he'll fight, and if I don't kill him, you will?"

"You're a sharp one, bucko. I always said that."

"But why you, old man? There's nothing in it for you, except maybe getting your job back."

"That's no small thing to me," Kane said. "But it's not for my job I want to see Harbeson dead. He's gone too far. For one thing, he used a fist on me. For another, he won't let Mrs. Forbes leave Crescent. And besides, I've come to figure that so long as that bastard lives this country will go on being a no man's land—and that's got to come to an end."

He went out on that.

And as the door closed behind Kane, Jake Maugher said, "Bannister, he's as crazy as you. I want no part of it after I've said my piece to

Vorhees. I'm going to run for it, then, and you're not going to stop me."

"Quit worrying, Jake," Bannister said. "After you've been heard at Crescent you can run as fast as you can and as far as you want."

"There's one thing more, damn you."

"Well, get it said—and then shut up."

Surprisingly, Jake Maugher laughed. And said, "You're a crazy galoot, but a man's got to admire you. You know, Bannister, I kind of wish you luck."

"That's something I'll probably need plenty of," Bannister said. "And you too."

They ate supper with the Maurys, then saddled their horses and rode out. Luck was not with them, however. The moon had risen in full in a cloudless sky, and so they lacked darkness for cover. Just outside of Dalton, they came face to face with two riders. In the bright moonlight, Bannister recognized Clay Roland and old Jess Tolliver, two of the men he'd met at the Ranchers' League meeting. As he and Jake Maugher lifted their horses to a run, he heard old Tolliver burst out, "Damn me, that was Bannister and one of the Maughers!"

Looking back, Bannister saw that the pair had stopped and were staring after him and Jake.

The two ranchers didn't come after them, but a couple of miles farther on, Bannister sighted a group of horsemen heading toward town. With Jake, he left the road and headed south across the range. They turned toward Crescent again only when Bannister felt sure that the riders hadn't come after them. He hoped they were Crescent hands. The fewer men at Crescent when he arrived, the better it would be for him.

They came within sight of Crescent head-quarters at about eleven o'clock. Despite the lateness of the hour, several downstairs windows of the ranch house glowed with lamplight. Bannister kept a closer watch on Jake Maugher now, knowing the man's fear of Matt Harbeson might drive him to make a break. He drew his gun and let Jake see it in his hand.

They circled around behind the ranch house. There was no cover for their horses, so they dismounted and left them ground-hitched a hundred yards from the house. Taking his rifle with him, Bannister peered warily about the buildings. He saw neither Crescent men nor Jubal Kane. The bunkhouse was dark, its door closed. Only in the house did there seem to be anyone still awake. His luck had turned wholly sour, it seemed. Kane must have failed to find Will Langley and Pat Keough at Rawson Wells, and then changed his mind about being in on the showdown. Bannister felt a sharp disappoint-ment. He'd hoped he wouldn't need to play out the final hand alone.

They reached the rear door and found it unlocked.

Bannister pushed it open. He said, "Ahead of me, Jake."

He followed Jake into and through the unlighted kitchen, then along the hall to the front of the house. The parlor was lighted, and before they reached its doorway, Helen called, "Who's there?" in a voice sharp with alarm.

They reached the doorway, Bannister, pushing Jake in ahead of him. He said, "Jim Bannister, Mrs. Forbes."

She'd been reading, and now she rose from her chair so abruptly that her book fell to the floor. She said, "Jim—Jim!" and something in her voice caused a ripple of excitement to course through him. It was as though the sight of him filled her with a sudden happiness. She took a step toward him, then saw Jake Maugher and halted. Her expression changed to one of wonder.

"What is it, Jim?" she said. "Why have you come here?"

"This man saw John Forbes murdered," he told her. "I brought him here to tell that to Vorhees. Where is Vorhees, Helen?"

"He went to his room several hours ago."

"How about getting him down here?"

She started toward the door.

He said, "Is Matt Harbeson around?"

She spun around, quick fury in her eyes. "He

rode out just before dark. Toward Dalton. He's still searching for you, and he's been like a wild man the past several days. He's moved into this house. He treats Mr. Vorhees as if he owned Crescent Ranch and the old gentleman was a trespasser. He acts as if he hates everything and everybody. I think his failure to hunt you down is making a madman of him."

"He's molested you?"

"No. He just won't let me leave."

"Well, it'll soon be over."

Helen nodded, but the glow his arrival had brought to her face was replaced by a troubled expression. "I'm not sure he'll accept this as his downfall, Jim," she said. "I don't think he'll ever admit defeat. And if he should come while you're here—" She shuddered. "I'll get Mr. Vorhees."

She hurried from the room.

Bannister began a restless pacing, and Jake Maugher watched him anxiously. Both knew that Matt Harbeson might return to the ranch at any moment. The group of riders they'd seen headed toward Dalton had been Harbeson and some of the Crescent crew. Upon arriving in town, they certainly would have heard from Jess Tolliver and Clay Roland that they'd seen Bannister and Maugher riding toward Crescent. By now Harbeson would be on his way to Crescent, with murder in his heart. Bannister stopped pacing, looked at Jake.

"After we've talk to Vorhees, you clear out," Bannister told Jake. "Save yourself."

"What about you?"

"I'm taking Mrs. Forbes away from here."

"You'll never make it, Bannister."

Bannister gave him a probing look. He'd given Jake a rough time of it. His gun had killed Jake's brother, Russ. But somehow during the days and nights since Bannister took him away from Red Sorensen's place, Jake had got over his hatred and now offered a grudging friendliness. Bannister saw that Jake's concern was genuine.

He said, "Maybe I won't make it, Jake. But I've got to try."

Helen returned. She said Mr. Vorhees had awakened when she knocked on his door and had promised to come down. She added, "There's one thing you should know, Jim. Harbeson has lied to him about me. He's convinced Mr. Vorhees that you and I—well, that you killed John because of me. You see, he's so influenced by Harbeson that nothing I could say in your defense made any difference."

"Well, he won't be influenced by Harbeson now," Bannister said. "I'll make him see things straight, somehow."

The minutes ticked away. A quarter of an hour passed before they heard Vorhees on the stairs. When he finally entered the parlor, they saw that he'd taken time to make himself presentable even to collar, tie and coat. He was older than Bannister had imagined, not old in the rugged fashion of Jubal Kane, but frail, with ebbing strength.

Yet, as Vorhees entered the room, Bannister sensed the iron will in that aged body. Vorhees looked at him in a challenging way, and said, "So you're the man who's caused all this trouble? You're Jim Bannister?"

"I'm Bannister, sir. And I'm here of my own free will. I didn't kill John Forbes, and it's important that you know that. You and everybody else in No Man's Land. This man—" he gestured toward Jake Maugher—"witnessed the killing. I've brought him here to tell you what he saw. Jake, get it said."

Jake started to speak in a croaking voice, then cleared his throat and managed to talk in a fairly unexcited way. He told what he'd seen at the Graveyard, much as he'd described it to Ben and Janet Maury. After he finished, Vorhees studied him at such length that Jake began to squirm.

"It's the truth, Mr. Vorhees," Jake said. "I wouldn't lie for Bannister. I've got no reason to love this Texan, I can tell you."

"You would swear to it?"

"Sure."

Vorhees said, "Helen, isn't there a Bible on that table?"

Helen got the leather-bound Scriptures from

the table. Without hesitation Jake Maugher lay his left hand upon it and raised his right hand. "I swear I saw it just like I said, so help me God."

Vorhees looked from one to another of them without speaking.

Bannister said, "Well, do you believe it?" His voice was curt now with impatience, with the edginess come of knowing that time was running out. "What do you say, sir?"

Before the old man could reply, they heard the clatter of hoofs. A bunch of riders had entered the ranchyard. Fear became a live thing in the room.

Bannister had been holding his rifle all this while. Now he levered a cartridge into its firing chamber.

"Jake, run for it."

Jake started for the door. He paused there. "Come along, man! Save yourself!"

Bannister shook his head. "I'm playing out my hand."

He heard Jake's boots pounding along the hall toward the kitchen. Then another man's boots racketed across the porch. The front door opened so violently that it flew back and struck the wall. A man appeared at the parlor doorway.

Matt Harbeson.

CHAPTER TWENTY-ONE

At sight of Matt Harbeson, Jim Bannister felt a sudden wicked pleasure, and for an instant he wanted to kill. But it wasn't in him to shoot a man down deliberately, even though the man was Matt Harbeson. He held his rifle steady, but his finger no longer exerted pressure on the trigger.

Harbeson uttered a short mocking laugh.

"That's your trouble, Bannister," he said. "There's a soft streak in you. I knew it. That's why I walked in on you."

He stood there arrogantly, his feet widespread and his thumbs hooked in his cartridge studded gunbelt. A big, rock-hard man, he regarded Bannister contemptuously for a moment longer, then looked at Helen and at old Vorhees. He sneered at them.

"Nobody got anything to say?"

Vorhees said, "There was a witness to John Forbes's murder, Matt."

"That's too bad. I'll have to take care of him."

"You don't seem to take this seriously," Vorhees said. "There is no law in the Neutral Strip, and therefore you can't be brought to trial. But you're through here at Crescent Ranch. You'll leave at once, and not return."

Harbeson looked at him with an ugly amusement. "You just don't savvy, old man," he said. "When you came here, I was scared of you. Of your money. But I've had time to figure it out. There's no need for me to be scared of you or of your millions." He glanced at Bannister. "You're the sharp one. Tell the old fool how it is."

Bannister felt sick at heart. Harbeson held the winning hand and meant to play the game out to the bitter end. He knew of only one way to stop him—the simplest way and, for himself, the hardest. He kept the Winchester trained on Harbeson, its stock solidly against his thigh, his finger on the trigger. The slug would tear through Harbeson before he could make a move to save himself. But Bannister was up against what Harbeson called a soft streak. He couldn't kill in cold blood, and Harbeson would never make it a fight. Bannister remained silent, his face bleak.

Harbeson said, "He's lost his tongue. So I'll tell you how it is, old man. I'm not leaving. I founded this ranch. I made it what it is. By damn, I *am* Crescent Ranch. If the rest of the stockholders back East want to go along with me, I'll play square with them. But let them meddle like you're meddling, and I'll show them what fools they were to invest money in No Man's Land— where there's no law or courts to protect their investment. The only law is what a man carries in his holster, old man, and it's not a law that favors a rich bastard like you." He looked back at Bannister. "Come out when you're ready," he said, and on that he whirled and strode from the room and from the house.

The front door slammed, leaving a taut silence behind it.

Then Helen gasped, "Jim."

"I'm sorry, Helen. I couldn't shoot him down, and that was my only chance."

"Get out the back way!"

"Too late. He'll be sending men around there now." He gazed at her briefly, etching the picture of her in his memory. Then he said, "I'll go out the front way. Maybe I can get him before they cut me down."

Vorhees said incredulously, "You think they'll shoot you, Bannister?"

"I know it."

"I won't permit it. I'll go out and talk to the men."

"They're Harbeson's men, Vorhees."

"They can't be murderers!"

Bannister said, "You don't understand. They're not murderers, not all of them, anyway. But it won't be murder, the way they see it. So far as they know, I killed John Forbes. And they'll feel justified in killing me. They're tough hands, and they think they're loyal to their outfit by doing as Harbeson tells them." He paused, wondering what Harbeson planned for old Vorhees. It wasn't likely that Harbeson would permit the old man to return East. He looked at Helen, feeling wretched because he'd failed her. But she seemed to be holding her head in a listening attitude, and he saw fright in her eyes. "What is it, Helen?"

"There's somebody in the house, Jim!"

He swung around, strode to the hall.

From the kitchen came the sounds of men feeling their way through the darkness. A shadowy figure emerged, and then he heard a hoarse whisper: "Jim? That you, Bannister?"

It was Jubal Kane, and Will Langley and Pat Keough were behind him.

Kane said, "We're a little late, bucko. At Rawson Wells I found out these two had just started out for Kansas. I lost a lot of time riding after them. What's going on here?"

Bannister told them, then added, "I've brought you three into a trap."

"Seems like it," Jubal agreed. "Just after we closed the kitchen door we heard some of the crew around back. They'll pick us off when we try to leave. There's no other way?"

Helen came from the parlor, carrying a small hand lamp. Vorhees followed her. She said, "There must be a way. Jim, Mr. Vorhees is going to talk to the men. I'm going out there with him and—"

"No!"

Kane said, "Let them go, Jim."

263

Bannister swung toward him. "You crazy, Jubal?"

"Harbeson's not going to harm Mrs. Forbes," Kane said. "I doubt if he'll bother Vorhees, with the crew looking on. He knows they wouldn't stomach that. And there's a good chance that some of them—maybe most—can be reasoned with. They're not all cutthroats, remember."

Helen said, "He's right, Jim. It's the only way."

"All right," Bannister said. "But I'm going with you."

He wouldn't be argued out of it. When Helen opened the door and stepped out onto the porch, Vorhees went after her. Bannister saw a bunch of saddled horses in the middle of the yard. Between them and the porch steps stood three men—Matt Harbeson, with Sanchez flanking him on one side and the hardcased kid, Sherry, on the other. Bannister counted seven horses out there, so he knew four men had gone behind the house. The bunkhouse was lighted now, and the rest of the crew, some only partially dressed but all armed, came from it. One of them asked, "Matt, what's up?" and another exclaimed, "By damn, there's Bannister!"

Bathed in moonlight and the glow from the two lighted buildings, as well as the lamp Helen held, Bannister knew he made an easily recognized, clear target. At the moment, however, Helen's presence kept the Crescent hands from opening fire. There was that to be said for them, Bannister reflected; they didn't want to endanger her.

Harbeson called out, "That's right, Bannister. Hide behind a woman's skirt!"

Helen's voice quivered but reached across the yard. "You men come closer. Mr. Vorhees has something to say."

"Never mind that," Harbeson said. "You, Bannister, come down here!"

Vorhees moved to the edge of the porch. "I intend to be heard," he said. "I want you men to hear me out. I've discharged Matt Harbeson because—"

Harbeson yelled, "Sanchez, get over there and shut him up!"

Sanchez leaped forward, his gun in his hand. Bannister fired a shot that came so close to Sanchez that he yelped and came to a dead stop. Bannister jacked another cartridge into the rifle's chamber.

"Next time it'll be right between the eyes, Sanchez," he said. "The old man is going to be heard."

Jubal Kane came from the house, followed by Will Langley and Pat Keough. At sight of them Sanchez took a backward step, and Matt Harbeson swore bitterly. Four men came around the corner of the house at a run, guns drawn, but they halted when they saw Bannister and three armed companions on the porch. Kane moved past Bannister and joined Vorhees at the steps.

"Like Bannister said, Mr. Vorhees is having his say," Kane told them. "It's either that or there'll be dead men here in Crescent ranchyard."

The kid, Sherry, could stand it no longer. In a loud and reckless voice, he said, "Matt, quit this fooling around! Let's put an end to it!"

Bannister pushed past Kane and Vorhees and went down the steps. "Kid, keep your big mouth out of this," he said, raging. "I had trouble with you the first day I came into this country, and I'll be damned if I'll have you make more for me. I'm warning you now, Sherry. One more word out of you and you'll not live to get dry behind the ears!" He was shouting, and he went on, "If I've got to do the talking here, I'll do it. There's the man who bushwhacked John Forbes. Yeah—Matt Harbeson. Now if you want a fight, let's have it!" His angry gaze swept from man to man, coming to a rest on Sherry there beside Harbeson. "What do you say, kid?"

Sherry looked rattled, and even the tough Sanchez appeared edgy. The others stared at Harbeson in a shocked way.

Harbeson stood motionless and silent, his gun hanging at his thigh.

It seemed to Bannister that something inside the man crumbled. He'd once seen a man gamble away his ranch in a poker game in San Antonio, and as that man rose from the deal table and went outside to put a bullet through his head, he looked much as Matt Harbeson did now. After a while, Harbeson holstered his gun and went to the horses. He caught one up. He missed the stirrup on the first try, then made it to the saddle. His shoulders sagged, and for a time he sat there with his head bowed.

Bannister said, "You two—Sanchez and Sherry—keep him company. There's nothing for you around here anymore."

They went willingly enough, and Sherry said, when they were mounted, "Matt, let's go. We can fix that bastard later. We can lay for him and—"

Sanchez said, "Shut up, you fool!"

Harbeson remained motionless a moment longer, then roused from his dazed condition. He lifted the reins, kneed his horse into motion. It had traveled only a few yards when he pulled it in. He stared at Bannister and the people on the porch.

"I founded this ranch," he said savagely. "I made it out of nothing. It's mine more than any man's, and I'll have what's mine. Mark my words, the lot of you—I'll be back!"

He rode across the yard, Sanchez and Sherry falling in behind him. Harbeson's outburst could have been bluster, a final show of bravado, but Bannister wasn't sure.

He said, "Jubal, get Mrs. Forbes and Mr. Vorhees inside—quick!"

His warning came too late. Reaching the edge of the yard, Harbeson shouted something to the other two. All three came wheeling about, with a blast of shots.

Bannister saw Jubal Kane collapse on the porch steps. He saw Will Langley leap forward, then stop suddenly as a slug found him. Pat Keough grabbed Helen and pulled her toward the doorway. He shouted wildly at Mr. Vorhees, but the old man stood frozen. The Crescent hands scattered for cover. Bannister saw all that as he swung around and jerked his rifle to his shoulder.

He too was a target for their guns, and slugs shrieked about him. He caught Sanchez in the Winchester's sights, and squeezed out his shot. His slug knocked Sanchez off his spooked and bucking horse. Sherry racked his mount with spurs, driving it at Bannister. The kid fired and missed, then tried another shot, but there was no report this time as the hammer of his revolver fell on a fired cartridge. The range was pointblank for Bannister, but he had to sidestep to keep from being ridden down, and the shot went wide. Sherry leaned from the saddle, clubbing with his gun. Bannister ducked. The blow missed his head, but clouted him on the shoulder with such force that it drove him to his knees.

Sherry wheeled his horse about. He swung in against Bannister as he rose. The animal's left shoulder struck Bannister's chest, sent him reeling. Sherry came after him again before he recovered his balance. He dropped his rifle and grabbed at the kid's arm as he struck another blow with his gun. He braced himself and jerked Sherry from his plunging horse. He dumped Sherry heavily to the ground, and then, as Harbeson's gun racketed, he dived for his rifle. Sherry came up fast and rushed at him, but the kid got between him and Harbeson's gun as Harbeson fired again. A scream ripped from Sherry's throat, then choked off. He collapsed beside Bannister and didn't move again.

Harbeson was still at the edge of the yard, and as Bannister kneeled to drive a shot at him, he swung his horse away in sudden flight. He twisted in the saddle and shouted, "I'll be back, Bannister! I'll be back!"

Bannister slammed another shot at him, missed, then rose and caught up Sherry's horse. He swung to the saddle, jabbed spurs to the animal, and went after Harbeson.

There was no wild desire for revenge in Jim Bannister as he started out after Harbeson. Actually, he'd had more than enough of gunplay and bloodshed. He didn't want to risk his life further. This was simply something that had to be done, this riding Harbeson down. He had to finish the fight now, or have it renewed in the future, at a time when Harbeson caught him off guard. He'd have been willing to call it quits, to let the man ride out, but Harbeson's "I'll be back, Bannister! I'll be back!" had been no idle threat. If he got away, Matt Harbeson would indeed return, waging war to take over Crescent Ranch.

Bannister didn't need to wonder how the man would be able to do that. Harbeson rode north, and only Rawson Wells lay to the north. Many of the Strip's outlaws hung around the Wells, and if Harbeson had the money, as no doubt he had, he could hire gunmen to side him, against Bannister. He had to be stopped, then, and the only way to stop Matt Harbeson was to kill him.

The country was table-flat and the moon bright, so Bannister could keep him in sight. But he couldn't shorten Harbeson's lead and bring him within rifle range. Mile after mile, Harbeson drove his horse at a hard run. Bannister could feel his mount's sides heaving, and feared it would play out soon. Finally its stride began to falter, and a savage anger got hold of him as he realized that the chase was about over for him. Then he saw Harbeson's horse go down. The man had ridden it to the ground.

He reined in, dismounted and left his blowing, lathered animal. He ran forward, covering a hundred yards, then halted and dropped to the ground. Harbeson had thrown himself clear of his downed horse and was picking himself up. The horse scrambled up too, but was so far gone that it just stood spread-legged with its head hanging to the ground. Harbeson jerked his rifle off the saddle and faced in Bannister's direction.

"All right, Bannister," he shouted. "This is as it should be!"

He stood there and drove shot after shot at Bannister, as rapidly as he could work lever and trigger. Bannister heard the shriek of the slugs. One kicked dirt into his face. Harbeson got out five fast, wild shots before Bannister, taking deliberate aim, finally fired. He had the crack of the shot in his ears, then heard a yelled oath from Harbeson. He saw the man stagger and fall. He readied another shot, but suddenly had no target. He rose warily, still unable to see his man. There on that grass flat Harbeson had managed to disappear. He must have dropped into a gully or an old Buffalo wallow.

Bannister had no feeling that he'd killed Harbeson, and he knew the wounded man could still be dangerous. For a long minute he didn't know what move to make next. Then he sank to the ground, lay down his rifle, drew his revolver and began to crawl. He set out to flank the spot where he'd last seen Harbeson, and he could keep his bearings by glancing occasionally at the man's motionless horse. He'd crawled through the grass for perhaps fifty yards when a rasping sound alerted him. After a moment he recognized it as labored breathing, breathing grown loud because of some obstruction in throat or nostrils. Harbeson was on the move, very close.

Bannister stretched out flat and tried to keep his own hurried breathing noiseless. He no longer heard Harbeson, but he knew the man was still near him—too near. Here he was, as he had been from the start, with Matt Harbeson pressing him, stalking him like a wounded mountain lion that refused to give up its prey. Bannister's hand gripped the butt of his gun until it ached. He had broken out in a clammy sweat. This was fear, and he admitted it.

Suddenly the man broke out in racking coughing, and the sound placed him off to Bannister's right. Bannister heaved over in a quick roll, and as he moved he saw the great shadowy shape of Harbeson rise from a gully barely ten feet away. Harbeson's gun blasted, its muzzle flash glaring in Bannister's eyes. Rolling again, Bannister fired from the ground. He missed. He scrambled to his feet, but now Harbeson was upon him. He could see the man's face, contorted by hatred—and perhaps by pain, for blood streamed from Harbeson's mouth. Bannister tried to sidestep, but Harbeson collided with him. The impact sent him reeling backward, and Harbeson slashed with his gun. The weapon's long barrel struck him along the left jaw. Pain blinded him and the blow drove him to his knees. Another blow landed, this one to his shoulder. He threw himself on his side, panicky now with the knowledge that Harbeson intended to beat him to death.

His vision cleared sufficiently for him to see the man towering above him, readying another blow. He heaved upward, threw himself against Harbeson's legs. Already unsteady from his wound, Harbeson staggered backward and Bannister, without coming erect, fired once and then again. The force of the slugs striking him drove Harbeson farther back. He managed to stop himself, and for one terrible moment he cursed Bannister with his last breath. Then at last he fell, dropping from Bannister's sight.

Harbeson lay in the gully along which he had crawled. Bannister holstered his own gun and picked up the dead man's. He broke it and examined the cartridges in the cylinder, and then knew why Harbeson had tried to club him to death. The man had lost his head at the critical moment; he'd forgotten to reload the fired chambers after riding away from Crescent. Bannister dropped the empty gun.

Matt Harbeson had had a weak spot after all.

Bannister rode slowly, and gray dawn obscured the stars by the time he reached Crescent Ranch. The yard was empty of men and horses now, and the bodies of Sanchez and Sherry had been removed. Both the main house and the bunkhouse showed lights, and Pat Keough came across the ranch house porch as Bannister reined in.

"You got him, Jim?"

"I got him."

"Good."

"Yeah, good."

Keough eyed him with quick curiosity. "You don't seem happy about it, bucko."

Bannister sighed heavily. "Dead men," he said. "What's there to be happy about, Pat? He just wanted too much. He didn't know where to stop. Aside from that, he was a damn good man. And the other two—they shouldn't be dead."

"They knew the game they played, the risks they took," Keough said. "All three of them knew. Don't have them on your conscience, Jim."

"He's lying in a gully five, six miles north of here," Bannister said. "Tell the Crescent hands to bring him in, will you?"

"Sure."

"How about Will and Jubal?"

"Will's got a nasty crease in his left side, and maybe a nicked rib or two. Jubal's got a bullet hole through his left forearm, but it didn't hit the bones. They're a tough pair. In a week or two they'll forget they stopped lead. We patched them up, me and Mrs. Forbes. They're bedded down in the bunkhouse. Old Vorhees told the crew that from now on Jubal's the Crescent ramrod."

"Good for Jubal."

"Jubal gave the crew orders to round up your J-Bar-B cattle and throw them back onto your Boot Creek range. Good for you too, eh?"

Bannister smiled. "Yeah. Good for me too, Pat."

"That ain't all," Keough said. "Jubal offered me a job—and I took it. I'm supposed to straw-boss the crew when they start rounding up your cattle tomorrow."

"Going to play it straight, Pat?"

"Yep."

"I'll be damned."

Keough grinned. Then he said, "The lady's waiting up for you, bucko. I was sitting with her in the kitchen, drinking tea. Tea—imagine that. You'd better go tell her it's over. She's been real worried, I can tell you."

Bannister's smile faded. He found himself half afraid to face Helen. Still, he would be less than a man if he didn't face her. He dismounted, climbed the porch steps and entered the house. He went back along the hall, and she stood waiting in the kitchen. Bannister found it no different. Wanting her was a torment. It got worse each time he saw her.

"Jim—"

"Yes, Helen."

"Pat kept saying you'd come back, but I was afraid."

"It's over. There's nothing to be afraid of now."

"But nothing is the same, Jim. The harm has been done."

He nodded. "That's true," he said. "But don't blame me too much. My coming into No Man's Land touched off all this killing, but I had a right to come and I didn't come looking for trouble. Try to believe that, Helen."

"I can't find it in me to blame you at all," she said. "This is your country and you've got to be as you are to survive. It wasn't John's country and he couldn't adapt himself, so he didn't survive. I understand that."

"Yes. It's no good for some people—for people like you and John."

"Jim."

"Yes?"

"Are you trying to convince yourself of something?"

He looked at her frowningly. "I suppose I am. I've got to convince myself that you're not for me, that we belong in different worlds. It's true. You don't belong here."

"I've gone through so much without going to pieces," Helen said. "I'm hardier than you think. I can adapt myself here. I have already. I'll be a stranger in a strange land, if I go back East." She straightened. "I'm not going back East. There's nothing there for me. I've talked it over with Mr. Vorhees, and he's offered to let me live in this house as long as I wish."

"I have nothing to offer you, Helen."

"You're in love with me. That's sufficient."

"I don't see it that way."

"I talked about you to Mr. Vorhees, too," she said. "He feels that Crescent Ranch should make things up to you, somehow. If a loan would make things look different to you, all you have to do is ask him for it."

His frown faded slowly. He said, "Helen, I can't believe this is happening to me. That you should want to share my life—"

"You came into my life the day I was learning to handle a team," she said. "Besides John, you're the only man who ever did enter it. He's been gone only a few weeks, and I can't push aside the memory of him this quickly. I'll never do away with the memory of him entirely, and I don't want to. But if you give me a little time. If you'll let me have a proper length of time . . ."

Bannister's arms ached for the feel of her. But he said, "I wouldn't have it otherwise, Helen," and he meant it and was content. In due time, she would be his.

ABOUT THE AUTHOR

Jack Barton (pseudonym for Joseph L. Chadwick) began his writing career in 1935 to escape from a 35¢-an-hour factory job. He has written many types of novels but is recognized as an expert on Western Americana, resulting in his having had more than 600 Westerns published.

Center Point Large Print
600 Brooks Road / PO Box 1
Thorndike, ME 04986-0001 USA

(207) 568-3717

US & Canada:
1 800 929-9108
www.centerpointlargeprint.com